Hi! I'm Stephanie Tanner. Wait till you hear what happened to me! I wanted to join the Flamingoes, the coolest group in school. Being a Flamingo means instant popularity! Only it wasn't as easy as I thought. . . .

Wait. Hold it. Before I tell you my story, there's something you should know about me.

I come from a *very* large family.

Right now there are nine people and a dog living in our house—and for all I know, someone new could move in at any time. There's me, my big sister, D.J., my little sister, Michelle, and my dad, Danny. But that's just the beginning.

Uncle Jesse came first. My dad asked him to come live with us when my mom died, to help take care of me and my sisters.

Back then, Uncle Jesse didn't know much about taking care of three little girls. He was more into rock 'n' roll. So Dad asked his old college buddy, Joey Gladstone, to help out. Joey didn't know anything about kids, either—but it sure was funny watching him learn!

Having Uncle Jesse and Joey around was like having three dads instead of one! But then something even better happened—Uncle Jesse fell in love. He married Becky Donaldson, Dad's co-host on his TV show, *Wake Up San Francisco*. Aunt Becky's so nice—she's more like a big sister than an aunt.

Next Uncle Jesse and Aunt Becky had twin baby boys. Their names are Nicky and Alex, and they are adorable!

I love being part of a big family. Still, things can get pretty crazy when you live in such a full house!

FULL HOUSE™
Stephanie

Phone Call from a Flamingo

Devra Newberger Speregen

A Parachute Press Book

A MINSTREL® BOOK

PUBLISHED BY POCKET BOOKS

New York   London   Toronto   Sydney   Tokyo   Singapore

This book is a work of fiction. Names, characters, places, and incidents are either products of the author's imagination or are used fictitiously. Any resemblance to actual events or locales or persons, living or dead, is entirely coincidental.

A MINSTREL PAPERBACK *ORIGINAL*

 A Minstrel Book published by
POCKET BOOKS, a division of Simon & Schuster Inc.
1230 Avenue of the Americas, New York, NY 10020

A Parachute Press Book
Copyright © 1993 by Lorimar Television, Inc.

ISBN: 0-671-88004-7

First Minstrel Books printing October 1993

10   9   8   7

A MINSTREL BOOK and colophon are registered trademarks of Simon & Schuster Inc.

Printed in the U.S.A.

Phone Call From a Flamingo

CHAPTER

1

◆　◀　▸　◆

"Oh, puh-leeeese!" Stephanie Tanner couldn't believe what she had to watch every morning. Resting her elbows on the kitchen table, she dropped her chin into her palms and stared in disgust as her little sister Michelle "made breakfast."

What Michelle was really making was a mess. She was grabbing handfuls of cereal from five different boxes and stirring them together in a large mixing bowl.

"Michelle, do you have to do that?" Stephanie asked.

Seven-year-old Michelle rolled her eyes at her older sister. "Do what?" she asked innocently. "I'm making breakfast."

1

Stephanie leaned in for a closer look. "Michelle, that's totally revolting!"

"Well, you don't have to eat any," Michelle announced, pouring close to half a carton of milk over her cereal. "You don't even have to watch."

"You're right," Stephanie said. "I don't." She turned away, brushing her long blond hair from her face. Then she looked for the hundredth time at her watch. What on earth was taking her older sister, D.J., so long?

Michelle looked up from her bowl. "What's the problem, Stephanie?"

"D.J. is the problem," Stephanie said between clenched teeth. "Ever since I started junior high, D.J. and I have walked to the bus stop together. But lately D.J. keeps me waiting for hours. What could possibly take her so long to get ready for school?"

"I don't know," Michelle said. "Do you want me to make you another breakfast?"

"Yuck—no way." Stephanie glanced into the mixing bowl, where one of the cereals had turned the milk a sickening shade of pink. "But thanks anyhow, Michelle."

Stephanie loved walking to the bus stop with D.J. because that was their chance to talk. Oh, sure, there were lots of other people in the house she could talk to. Her uncle Jesse and his wife, Aunt Becky, were *great* to talk to, but lately they were so busy running after their twin sons, Alex and Nicky, that they didn't have much time for Stephanie.

Then there was her father's friend Joey. He always had time to talk. But talks with Joey always ended up funny. After all, Joey was a comedian by profession.

And anyway, how could she possibly ask Joey or Uncle Jesse or even her father about boys? Or about kissing? She knew she could never get up the nerve.

Once more, Stephanie turned in the direction of the stairs. "D.J.!" she yelled. "Will you c'mon already? I've been waiting almost twenty-five minutes for you!"

Stephanie was quiet, listening for her sister's answer. Or, better yet, for the sound of her feet coming down the steps. But the sound she now heard coming from upstairs was neither of these. It was a hair dryer!

Oh, brother, Stephanie thought. *D.J. hasn't even dried her hair yet. Now I'll have to take the late bus for sure!*

3

Suddenly the hair dryer stopped and D.J. called downstairs, "Steph? I hope you're not waiting for me."

"You hope *what?*" Stephanie called back.

"Don't wait!" D.J. yelled. "I told you before, Steve is driving me to school today."

"You never told me that!" Stephanie yelled back. She looked at Michelle. "Did D.J. tell me that?"

With a mouth full of cereal, Michelle shrugged.

"Yes, I did!" D.J. shot back.

"Did not!"

"Did too!"

"Will you guys cut it out?" Michelle cried. "I can't eat with all this yelling." She picked up her bowl and stomped off to finish her cereal in the living room.

"Listen, Stephanie!" D.J. yelled from the top of the stairs. "I did tell you that Steve was driving me to school today." Her hairbrush in hand, she came halfway down the stairs. "Steve finally got his car back from the repair shop, and he promised to give me a ride. I'd ask you to come with us, Steph, but you know his car—only room for two. Anyway, I haven't seen Steve in two whole days. We need some time alone."

"Two whole days without seeing lover boy?" Stephanie said, her voice dripping with phony sympathy. "How did you stand it?"

"Give me a break, Steph," D.J. said.

"I mean, the guy is at our house practically every day," Stephanie went on. "Every minute you're not in school, you're with him, D.J. You don't have time for anybody else anymore!"

"That's not true!" D.J. insisted.

"Yes, it is!" Stephanie snapped. "Two weeks ago you promised to sort through all your old clothes and let me have the things you didn't want anymore. But have you done it? No way!"

"Steph, I've got heavy-duty homework! I haven't had time!"

"You found time to go to the movies with Steve!" Stephanie threw her lunch sack into her book bag. "And what about last night?"

"What about it?"

"You flipped out when I was looking for a highlighter pen."

"Steph! You were going through my desk drawers."

"Big deal! D.J., we used to share a bedroom. We shared a desk. Now, all of a sudden, your desk is off limits?"

5

"I need some privacy, Stephanie. Listen," said D.J., "we don't have time to discuss this right now. Why don't you go catch up with Kimmy and walk to the bus stop with her?"

"Kimmy Gibbler!" Stephanie rolled her eyes and made gagging noises. "She may be your best friend, D.J., but she's the last person I'd ever walk to school with. For one thing, that girl never stops talking. No, thank you." Stephanie reached for her book bag and stormed out of the house, making sure to slam the door behind her.

Stephanie strode toward the bus stop, still fuming at her sister. She was so lost in her own thoughts that she hardly saw where she was going. So what if D.J. spent all her time with Steve. Who cared? She was nothing but a big crank and a privacy freak anyway. When Stephanie and D.J. had shared a room, before Stephanie moved in with Michelle, there hadn't been any of these privacy problems. She and D.J. used to stay up incredibly late and have great talks about boys. All Michelle ever wanted to talk about was coloring!

And this morning Stephanie really needed

D.J.'s advice. She'd wanted to ask D.J. what she should do about her major crush on Brandon Fallow. Brandon Fallow—just thinking his name gave her chills. He was the cutest boy in the eighth grade, tall with straight dark hair and dark eyes, star of the soccer team, totally popular . . . and he didn't know Stephanie existed.

By the time Stephanie got to school, it was already past eight o'clock. She'd had to take the late bus, so she'd missed seeing her best friends, Allie and Darcy. When one of them missed the bus in the morning, they met at the pay phone by the gym—but now it was even too late for that. Groaning, Stephanie hurried to homeroom. Thanks to D.J., her day was off to a rotten start!

It wasn't until lunchtime that Stephanie finally saw Allie, sitting at their usual table in the cafeteria. Stephanie had known Allie Taylor since the first day of kindergarten, where, since they both had last names beginning with *T*, they were seated next to each other. Allie was a small girl with long, wavy light brown hair and pretty green eyes. Stephanie hurried toward the table. She couldn't wait to sit down and spill out all her worries to her best friend. Allie was one of the most sensible people Stephanie knew.

"I waited for you by the pay phone until eight o'clock," said Allie. "Is everything okay?"

Stephanie tossed her brown lunch bag onto the table and fell into a chair. "Not really," she said.

"What is it, Steph? You can tell me."

"It's . . . well . . . it's just that lately D.J.'s been totally ignoring me," Stephanie said, feeling lucky to have a best friend she could trust to always listen. "Everything is Steve, Steve, Steve! It's really getting on my nerves. And today I waited the whole morning to walk to the bus stop with her, and then she rode to school with Steve. I mean, how rude!"

"Really!" Allie smiled reassuringly at her friend. "But maybe D.J. just needs some space," she added sympathetically.

Stephanie slumped down farther in her chair. "Yeah, I guess," she agreed halfheartedly. "At least I have my friends. Do you want to come over after school this afternoon?"

Allie was about to answer when Darcy Powell came running over to the table and dropped down into the chair across from them. Darcy had moved to San Francisco from Chicago less than a year before, and Stephanie and Allie had liked her right away. The three had become great friends. Darcy was a tall, slim, and graceful African-American girl. Some people said Darcy looked like Whitney Houston, but whenever they said so, Darcy laughed and said, "I wish!"

"Guess what!" Darcy announced breathlessly.

"What?" Stephanie and Allie asked in unison.

"You'll never, ever, ever, *ever* guess what happened!"

"What?" Stephanie asked. "Darcy, what? You really want us to guess?"

Darcy laughed. "You'd never guess anyway. Not in a million years! Not in a trillion! Not in a—"

"Just get to it!" Stephanie snapped. She wasn't exactly in the mood for any more fooling around today.

"Okay," Darcy said. "Here goes. A little while ago, Jenni Morris invited *me*, Darcy Powell, to join the Flamingoes!"

Stephanie opened her mouth, but nothing came out. She was speechless.

9

"The Flamingoes?" Allie asked.

Darcy nodded, grinning from ear to ear.

Stephanie found her voice. "You're going to get to go to all their cool parties? And all their great sleep-overs?"

Again Darcy nodded.

"And you'll start wearing something pink to school every day?" Stephanie asked. "Just the way the other Flamingoes do?"

"Yes!" squealed Darcy.

"And sit at their cafeteria table?" Stephanie asked. "And have a cool boyfriend? And paint the nail of your pinkie finger—"

"Hold it, hold it," interrupted Allie. "The girls in the Flamingoes club are seventh and eighth graders. You're only in sixth. I mean, I'm really happy for you and all, but why did they pick *you?*"

Darcy folded her arms across her chest. "Excuse me, Allie Taylor, but what's that supposed to mean?"

"I know what she means, Darcy," Stephanie said. "It *is* kind of weird. I mean, don't you think so? You being the only sixth grader in the entire school asked to join the Flamingoes?"

Darcy stood up and put her hands on her

hips. "No," she said angrily. "I don't think it's weird. I think you're just jealous!"

Before Stephanie could answer, Allie shot her a look that said *chill out*. Stephanie knew Allie was right. She ought to be happy for her friend. "Yeah, Darcy," she said as cheerfully as she could manage, "this is totally cool news. Exactly what did Jenni Morris say?"

Darcy looked at Stephanie a bit suspiciously, but she was bursting to tell all the details. "Well, Jenni was waiting for me by my locker right after second period, and she handed me this little pink note." Darcy slipped the note out of a book and handed it to Allie. Stephanie read it over her shoulder.

Darcy Powell,

How would you like to become a member of the ultimate, ultracoolest club in school? Come to our official Flamingoes meeting tomorrow after school at my house and we'll talk about letting you try out.

> Catch ya later!
> Yours forever pink,
> Jenni Morris
> President of the Flamingoes

As Stephanie stared at the pink ink on the pink paper, she ached with wishing that the name on the top of the letter were not *Darcy Powell* but *Stephanie Tanner*. Oh, how could Darcy be so lucky? Now she'd be instantly popular! She'd be friends with the older, cooler kids. Oh, if only she, Stephanie Tanner, had been invited to be in the Flamingoes, then she wouldn't have to worry about liking Brandon Fallow. He'd automatically be superinterested in her—a real, live Flamingo!

CHAPTER
2

◆ ◀ ◆ ◆

Later that afternoon, Stephanie headed for her locker to get her textbook before her science class started.

As she approached her locker, Stephanie noticed something pink sticking out from one of the air slots. It was a folded-up note! She broke into a run. Maybe it was . . . Could it be? Quickly she snatched the note and opened it.

Dear Stephanie,
   I forgot to tell you—I can't go to your house after school today. I've got to meet with Ms. Burns about the play we're doing

in English. Sorry about that—I'll call you tonight.

Y.B.F.,
Allie

Letting out the breath she'd been holding, Stephanie pressed her lips together and crumpled up Allie's note in her hand. What a letdown! What a disappointment! How could Allie be so . . . so *dumb* as to use pink stationery! Jenni Morris and the Flamingoes practically owned the color pink! Didn't Allie understand anything? Stephanie glanced again at the way Allie had signed her note: Y.B.F., which was their code for Your Best Friend. *Well, right now, Allie,* thought Stephanie, *I wouldn't sign a note to you that way!*

Clutching the note tightly in her hand, Stephanie raced down the hall to science class. Luckily she made it to the classroom just as Mr. Machlin was closing the door. Whew! That was close! One more late mark from Mr. Machlin and she'd be in a lot of trouble. She slid into her seat and waited for roll call to start.

After science, Stephanie headed for history. As she passed the science lab on her way down

14

the hall, she spotted Allie pacing nervously outside. Allie was chewing her fingernails and
peering through the glass panel in the door
every couple of seconds.

Stephanie came up behind her. "Seen Adam
yet?"

Allie jumped. "Oh, Steph!" she gasped. "You
startled me." Then, dropping her voice to a
whisper, she added, "And don't say his name
out loud around me, okay? Somebody might
hear and then . . ."

"And then they'd know," Stephanie said, not
whispering at all, "that you have the world's
biggest crush on Adam Green, who has seventh-
grade science lab right here every Monday,
Wednesday, and Friday, fifth period."

"Steph!" Allie whispered, sounding hurt.
"Cut it out!"

"I'm sorry," Stephanie said. "I'm just feeling—I don't know, sort of mad."

"About what?" Allie asked, darting another
glance into the science lab, where the seventh
graders were gathering up their books.

"About the note," Stephanie replied. "The
one you left in my locker."

"Why would *that* make you mad?" Allie

asked, freezing as still as a statue. Adam and one of his friends came out of the lab, laughing and fooling around. Stephanie wondered if she should tell Allie what she'd heard: that Adam Green was the off-again, on-again boyfriend of Diana Rink . . . Jenni Morris's best friend!

"It isn't your fault." Stephanie sighed. "I thought it might be from the Flamingoes."

"Oops!" Allie said. "I guess I shouldn't have used pink paper, huh?"

"Guess not," said Stephanie.

"But I don't see how you can actually be mad at me for that," Allie protested as the two girls headed down the hallway together.

"I'm not mad at you. I'm disappointed," Stephanie explained. "I mean, if I were a Flamingo, then Brandon Fallow might notice me."

"You really think so?" Allie asked.

"Yes!" Stephanie practically shouted. "Brandon hangs out with the Flamingoes!" Didn't Allie get it? She didn't seem to understand how great being in the Flamingoes would be.

If only I were a Flamingo, Stephanie thought with a sigh, *everything would be absolutely perfect.*

16

CHAPTER
3

◆ ◀ ▶ ◆

That night at dinner, the Tanner kitchen was overflowing with talking, laughing family members, as usual. Stephanie looked at the eight other people seated around the table. There was D.J., Michelle, their father, Joey, Uncle Jesse, Aunt Becky, and Nicky and Alex. It was almost as noisy and crowded as the school cafeteria!

"Hey, Nicky," Uncle Jesse said, holding a forkful of green beans up to his own mouth. "Look at Daddy. Mmm, beans! Yummy!"

Stephanie laughed at the look on Uncle Jesse's face—it was obvious that he, too, hated the green beans.

"Becky," Jesse whispered with a sour expression, "why don't you give it a try? I can't stand green beans."

Little Alex seemed to agree with his father. He turned his plate upside down onto the floor, crying, "Blah!"

Immediately Stephanie's father jumped up from the table, grabbed a damp sponge, and rushed over to Alex's side. He got down on all fours and began wiping the floor.

"Can't have them just lying around," Danny Tanner said when he noticed that everyone was watching him crawl around on his knees. "They'll start to get hard and stick to the floor, and then it'll be a real mess."

"Don't worry, Dad," Michelle said. "Comet will get them."

Stephanie giggled, picturing their family dog licking the green beans off the floor. "Maybe Comet won't like them either," she joked.

"Boy, Danny, you are a cleaning maniac," Joey said. "Ever thought of starting your very own line of cleaning products?"

"Right," Jesse said, getting in on the jokes. "The Danny Tanner Cleaner-Uppers!"

Suddenly the back door flew open and in walked D.J.'s boyfriend, Steve.

"Hey," Joey said. "It's the eating machine!"

"Perfect timing," Danny said sarcastically. "Steve, how in the world did you know that we were just sitting down to have dinner?"

Steve shrugged and pulled up a chair to the Tanner table.

"He must have smelled the chicken roasting all the way over at his house!" Michelle called out. Everybody laughed.

Danny finished cleaning the floor. After washing his hands thoroughly, he came back over to the table, picked up the large platter of roasted chicken, and set it down right in front of Steve. "Okay, so here's your dinner. What are the rest of us having?"

Steve turned a little red with embarrassment. "Well, it does smell great, Mr. T.!" he said, grabbing a piece of chicken.

"Help yourself," Danny said.

"He already has!" Joey and Michelle said at the exact same time.

Only Stephanie didn't join in the joking about Steve and his eating habits. Right now she just couldn't see any humor in D.J.'s boyfriend.

A few minutes later, D.J. stood up from the table. "Well, it's been real," she said. "Steve and I are going to watch some television." Then she took Steve's hand and led him toward the living room. "Thanks for dinner, Dad."

"Yeah, thanks, Mr. T.," Steve said, still munching on a chicken leg that was in his other hand. "It's been real."

"Uh, you're welcome," Danny said. "And, Steve," he added, "take a napkin for that drumstick."

Not to be left out, Michelle hopped off her chair too. "It's been real . . ." Then she stopped. "What does that mean?" she asked, looking confused. "It's been real *what?*"

Joey scooped her up and carried her upstairs to play. "We're not too sure, Michelle, but it seems to be the hip thing to say. Later, dudes," he added in his best Popeye voice. "It's been real! Right, Olive?"

"Right, Popeye!" Michelle replied in a not-so-great Olive Oyl voice.

Before Danny Tanner could say a word, everyone else began to get up. Stephanie took her plate to the sink and then followed D.J. and Steve into the living room.

On the couch, D.J. was lying with her head on a pillow in Steve's lap. With her long legs stretched out, she was taking up most of the sofa. But Stephanie didn't let this stop her from wedging her body into the small amount of room that was still left.

"Move your legs over, D.J.," she whined. "I need some space."

But D.J. didn't move her legs. She and Steve were giggling about something, and D.J. didn't pay any attention to Stephanie at all.

"What's so funny?" Stephanie asked.

"Nothing, nothing," D.J. said, covering Steve's eyes so he couldn't see the TV. "You wouldn't understand."

"Oh, I can understand quite a lot," Stephanie said, trying to cover up her hurt feelings. "You'd be surprised."

But D.J. and Steve continued to laugh and joke around, ignoring her.

"Really," Stephanie continued in a loud voice, "I understand loads. You have no idea just how much I understand! In fact, today in history class Ms. Field pointed out that I got one of the highest scores on our Civil War test, just like I did on our Revolutionary War test. And if I understood the whole Civil War *and* the whole Revolutionary War, I could probably understand what you're laughing about, don't you think? We haven't gotten around to studying any of the world wars yet, but I'm sure I'll understand—"

"Steph!" D.J. interrupted. "What in the world are you talking about?" She and Steve were looking strangely at Stephanie.

Stephanie stopped talking. She knew she hadn't been making a lot of sense. But who cared? At least she'd gotten D.J.'s attention.

"Hey, Deej, guess what!" she asked, thinking she would certainly be able to keep her sister's attention with her news about Darcy and the Flamingoes.

"What, Steph?" D.J. asked in a distracted way. Then she sat up on the couch and said, "Hey, Steve, where's the remote control? I know you have it. Come on! Give it to me!"

Stephanie had to dodge her sister's right elbow as D.J. leaned over to pry Steve's arm from behind his back.

Steve looked at his girlfriend with big, innocent eyes. "Remote?" he asked. "What remote? I don't know what you're talking about. I guess we'll just have to watch this Forty-niners game."

D.J. groaned loudly. "No way! I'm not sitting through another boring baseball game."

Steve laughed. *"Football*, Deej. The Fortyniners are a football team."

Stephanie rolled her eyes. "Even I knew that," she said, though no one was listening.

"D.J.," she tried again, "guess what? Darcy was asked to join the Flamingoes!"

"Steve, for the last time," D.J. cried. "Give me the remote control!"

"D.J., did you hear me?" Stephanie demanded angrily. "I said Darcy was asked to try out for the Flamingoes! You know, the coolest girls' club in school?"

But D.J. didn't answer. She was too busy tickling Steve and poking her arm under the couch cushions, searching for the TV remote.

"So isn't that great?" Stephanie continued, getting the feeling that she was talking to herself. "About Darcy, I mean. Can you imagine . . . I'm going to be friends with a real Flamingo. It's just so cool. And who knows? Maybe she'll get the Flamingoes to ask *me* to join." Knowing that her words were not being heard, Stephanie raised her voice over D.J. and Steve's giggling. "Yup! Really cool!" she shouted. "The Flamingoes! Darcy said that Jenni Morris came over to her locker today and—"

Abruptly D.J. stopped tickling Steve. "Wait a minute, Steph. Did you say something about Jenni *Morris?*"

Stephanie pretended to be shocked. "Oh! Did you actually hear what I was saying?" She smiled, feeling pleased that, just as she'd suspected, the mere mention of the popular Jenni Morris's name would make her sister take notice. "And are you actually talking to me?"

"Yes, I'm talking to you," D.J. said. "What did you say about Jenni Morris?"

"Only that Darcy, one of my best friends," Stephanie began proudly, "has started hanging around with Jenni. I just know Jenni and I are going to become great friends."

Steve started to tickle D.J. again, but D.J. pushed his hand away. "Time out, Steve," she said, switching the channel back to the football game. "I have to talk to Stephanie for a sec." She turned to her sister. "Steph," she said seriously, "Jenni Morris is Susan Morris's sister, right?"

"Right." Stephanie nodded. She'd forgotten

that Jenni had an older sister who was a junior in high school, like D.J.

"Listen, Steph," D.J. said. "Jenni Morris is not the kind of girl you should be hanging around with."

"Are you kidding?" That wasn't at all what Stephanie had expected to hear. "What do you mean?" she asked, confused. "Jenni is one of the most popular girls in school."

"Susan Morris is really bad news, Stephanie," said D.J. "I've heard all kinds of stuff about her—how she cuts school, hangs around with a bad crowd, and how she can be totally nasty. I don't know Jenni personally, but I've heard from kids I trust that she's just like her sister. If that's true, then she is definitely bad news too, and not the type of girl you should start hanging around with."

Stephanie stood and put her hands on her hips. "I can't believe what I'm hearing," she said. "Just because she has a rotten older sister, I shouldn't hang out with her? Do you think *I* should be judged by what *you* do in school?"

"I'm not saying that," D.J. protested. "I'm just saying you should watch out. Maybe Jenni isn't like her sister at all. But maybe she is. And if she is, then you don't want to get messed up with her and her crowd. And Darcy'd be crazy to get messed up with them, too."

"Darcy is the luckiest girl I know," Stephanie snapped at her sister. "It's an honor for a sixth grader to be asked to join the Flamingoes. You're the one who's crazy!"

"Stephanie, why are you getting so upset?" D.J. demanded. "I'm only trying to help you. I don't know what the big deal is about the Morris sisters anyway. Why does everybody think they're so cool?"

"Oh! So that's it!" Stephanie shouted.

"What's it?" D.J. asked.

"I see what's going on here, D.J. You don't like Susan or Jenni because they're so pretty and popular. You're jealous!"

D.J. laughed out loud. "Oh, please. Give me a break!" she cried, her voice growing louder and louder. "Why would I be jealous of a creepy class cutter and a stupid eighth grader?"

"Because you were never asked to join a club as cool as the Flamingoes, that's why!" Stephanie knew she was being pretty obnoxious, but it kind of felt good to put down D.J. *She deserves it anyway*, Stephanie thought, *for the horrible way she's been acting.*

"I would never want to join any club with Susan Morris in it," D.J. shot back. "Or Jenni either. You and Darcy are just asking for trouble!"

"Whoa! Wait a minute. Both of you. Calm down!" Steve jumped up from the couch and stood between the sisters. "C'mon, D.J., this is silly. Let's get out of here for a while and give everyone a chance to calm down."

D.J. looked back and forth between Stephanie and Steve. Then, with a final glare at her younger sister, she stormed out the front door, with Steve following her.

Stephanie picked up a pillow and slammed it down on the arm of the couch just as her father came into the living room.

"What's going on, Steph?" he asked. "It sounds like World War One in here."

"Oh, Dad!" Stephanie moaned. "Couldn't you have said the Civil War? Or the Revolutionary War? Why'd you have to go and pick a war that I know absolutely nothing about?" And with that, she turned and stomped up the stairs to her room.

"Huh?" Danny looked puzzled. "What'd I say?" he asked Comet, who was lying on the floor. "What'd I say?"

Stephanie was in such a bad mood, she had trouble concentrating on her homework that night. If she had to rate the way she felt on a scale of 1 to 10, she thought a 1.5 would be about right. Nothing was going her way in her life. Absolutely nothing!

When she heard the phone ring, Stephanie stopped reading and listened. Someone picked it up after the second ring.

"Stephanie!" Michelle called from the living room. "Phone for you!"

Even those three magical words, "Phone for you!" didn't make Stephanie feel any better. *It's probably Allie*, she thought, *wanting to tell me something about the play she's doing for English class. Or Darcy with more news about her new, older, cool friends.*

Stephanie went downstairs and took the receiver from Michelle's hand. Without much enthusiasm she said, "Hello?"

"Is this Stephanie Tanner?" came a voice on the other end.

"That's me."

"Stephanie, this is Jenni Morris."

Stephanie's mouth opened, but no words came out. Could this be happening to her? Could Jenni Morris really and truly be on the other end of the phone? Was she actually getting a phone call from a Flamingo?

"Hello? Stephanie? Are you there?"

"Uh, yeah . . . I'm here, Jenni. I'm right here."

"Good. Listen, I was wondering, would you like to come to a meeting tomorrow after school?"

"Yes!" Stephanie nearly shouted into the phone. "I mean, yes, I think I could do that. Let me look at my schedule." Stephanie held her hand over the receiver, counted to ten, and then said, "Uh, tomorrow looks okay."

"Great! Just come over to my house right after school and we'll talk about letting you try out for the Flamingoes. Darcy Powell's coming too. You know where I live. Oops! Got to run. Catch ya later!"

"Catch ya later," Stephanie said, even though she knew Jenni had already hung up. For a moment Stephanie just stood where she was, the phone in her hand, hoping that she was not having some sort of elaborate daydream. She'd gotten a phone call from Jenni Morris, and now everything was going to be just perfect. The sleep-overs, the cool table at lunch, the neat friendship bracelets, finding something pink to wear every day. And to top it off, the total attention of Brandon Fallow! He hung out with the Flamingoes—so he'd definitely hang out with her. If she became a Flamingo, nothing would ever go wrong in her life again.

CHAPTER

4

◆ ◂ ◂ ◆

The next morning Stephanie once again missed meeting Allie and Darcy on the bus and at the pay phone before school. But this time it wasn't D.J.'s fault that Stephanie was running late. Stephanie had been trying on just about every item in her closet, searching for the coolest possible outfit to wear over to Jenni's house. She finally settled on her jean skirt and a lavender T-shirt.

At lunchtime Stephanie hurried over to her usual cafeteria table, where Allie was already sitting.

"Allie," Stephanie said as she took a seat beside her friend, "did you happen to . . . to get a phone call from anyone interesting last night?"

When Allie looked thoughtful, as if trying to remember, Stephanie knew that the answer was no.

"Why?" Allie asked in between bites of her ham-and-cheese sandwich. "Did you? Did Brandon call you?"

"No," Stephanie said. "Not Brandon. Someone even better."

"Better than Brandon?" Allie almost spilled her carton of orange juice when she heard that. "Who? Who? *Who?*"

Stephanie took a deep breath. "Jenni Morris!" she announced. "She called me last night and asked me to try out for the Flamingoes!" She anxiously waited for Allie's reaction.

Allie put down her sandwich. She looked as though she'd just been kicked in the stomach.

Stephanie didn't know what to do to make her friend feel better, so she just kept talking. "Jenni asked me to come to her house this afternoon to talk about joining."

Allie was silent.

"Allie? Say something! Are you mad?"

Allie looked down at her sandwich as she shook her head. "Don't worry about it, Steph,"

32

she said. "It's okay. I mean, I'm not gonna get all depressed and everything just because the Flamingoes didn't ask me to join their club. I'm happy for you."

Then Allie went back to eating her sandwich, and it grew uncomfortably quiet at their table. Stephanie felt relieved when the fourth-period bell rang and lunch was over.

When the end-of-school bell rang that afternoon Stephanie rushed out of her last class, made a fast stop at her locker, and ran to the pay phone. She nearly collided with Darcy, who was zooming toward the pay phone from the opposite direction. During gym they had agreed to meet there, when Stephanie had told Darcy the good news.

"Ready?" Darcy asked breathlessly.

"Ready," Stephanie replied. "Here we come, Flamingoes!"

As the two girls walked out the double front doors of the school and headed toward Jenni's house, Stephanie asked, "You think Jenni might call Allie tomorrow? I mean, about becoming a Flamingo?"

"Who knows?" Darcy said. "I sure hope so.

Do you think they have a rule about how many sixth graders they can take?"

"I don't know," Stephanie said slowly. She didn't really want to think about Allie right now, or worry about her getting a call from the Flamingoes. She just wanted to bask in the happiness of her phone call from Jenni, and to enjoy every single second on her way to full-fledged Flamingo-hood.

Moments later, Stephanie could hardly believe she was sitting in Jenni Morris's very own bedroom with Jenni herself and Diana Rink, two of the most popular girls in school. She couldn't help but notice how sophisticated and mature they both looked. They were even wearing makeup!

Stephanie saw that Jenni and Diana were also wearing their official lavender-and-pink Flamingo friendship bracelets. Boy, she would give her right arm for one of those! Of course, then, she thought with a giggle, she'd have to wear the bracelet on her left wrist!

Even more awesome was the fact that both Jenni and Diana had their pinkie nails painted bright pink. Stephanie could hardly wait until the day she could show up at school wearing a pair of pink-painted pinkie nails, a Flamingo trademark.

Trying to act as casual as possible, Stephanie stole a glance over at Darcy. Darcy looked completely ecstatic. She'd even had the nerve to wear a pink T-shirt and pink sneakers for the occasion. Stephanie had thought maybe it wouldn't be right for her to wear pink before she had been made an official Flamingo; that's why she'd settled on lavender. But Jenni and Diana hadn't even seemed to notice that Darcy was decked out a little early in the official Flamingo color.

"Check out these new Doc Martens." Jenni's loud voice interrupted Stephanie's thoughts, bringing her back to what was taking place in Jenni's bedroom.

"Oh, Jenni," Diana said. "Those are only the most amazing pair of shoes I have ever seen. I swear, that green is just too much!"

Stephanie smiled, pretending to be interested. She didn't particularly like the look of the clunky shoes, but she didn't want to seem like a nerd by saying so. She hoped Doc Martens weren't the official Flamingo footwear, so that she wouldn't have to shell out about six months' allowance to buy herself a pair.

The two Flamingoes completely ignored the two sixth graders as they continued to discuss Jenni's new shoes and then moved on to the topic of Jenni's long-standing boyfriend, Mickey Parris, who had just moved to Boston. While the older girls talked to each other, Stephanie looked around Jenni's grown-up bedroom and began to feel even more nervous. Her own bedroom back home was so babyish compared to Jenni's. Sharing a room with Michelle didn't help matters, either. Michelle insisted on filling their room with dopy stuffed animals and pictures of kittens and puppies. No kittens or puppies adorned Jenni's walls. Instead, she had cool posters of Christian Slater and River Phoenix. Stephanie figured if Jenni liked those actors, they must be very cool.

When Jenni stopped talking for a second, Stephanie thought maybe she should say something—something cool, to impress the older girls. She turned to Jenni and said, "So you like Christian Slater?"

"Doesn't everybody?" Jenni replied.

"Oh, yeah, sure," Stephanie said. "I think

he's the greatest actor. I have lots of posters of him in my room at home." *At least I will as soon as I buy them and hang them up*, she added to herself.

"Cool," Jenni said.

Stephanie breathed a sigh of relief. Obviously what she'd said was okay.

Jenni stood up. "So . . . does anyone want a Diet Coke?"

"I'll take one," Diana answered.

"Me too," Darcy said.

"Sure," Stephanie said, grateful for something to drink. She was so nervous, her mouth had gone bone-dry.

Jenni reached under her desk and opened a tiny refrigerator. She pulled out four Cokes.

"Wow! You have your own fridge?" Stephanie asked in amazement. "That is so radical!" She couldn't imagine her father ever letting her keep a refrigerator, which might contain crumb-producing food, in her bedroom.

Secretly Stephanie prayed that she wouldn't ever have to hold a Flamingoes meeting at her house. She could just picture Jenni and the Flamingoes sitting around Michelle's little coloring table while Stephanie offered them fake tea from a dumb old play tea set! And she was sure that her father would embarrass her by coming in with his Dustbuster right in the middle of a meeting. Stephanie shuddered at the thought.

Finally Jenni said, "Flamingo time!" and officially began the meeting. "Stephanie and Darcy," she said in her most official-sounding, take-charge voice, "Diana and I have been selected by the Flamingoes as the Official Initiation Committee. We'll be in charge of making sure your initiation into the Flamingoes goes smoothly. We'll be sort of like your big sisters in the club, so if you have any questions at all, ever, you can come to us.

"As you know," she continued, "the Flamingoes have never let sixth graders into our club before, but we took a vote last week and decided to make an exception for you two girls."

As Jenni beamed her most terrific smile at the two sixth graders, Stephanie could hardly believe her good fortune.

"We all came to the conclusion," Jenni went on, "that the two of you seemed cool enough to give it a try."

Nearly limp with happiness, Stephanie smiled over at Darcy.

"But," Jenni went on, stressing the word *but*, "you're not Flamingoes yet. First you have to prove yourselves worthy of becoming Flamingoes and worthy of hanging around with us."

"Okay," Darcy said.

Stephanie nodded her agreement. "What do we do?"

Jenni darted a quick look at Diana. "All you have to do is successfully complete three harmless dares."

Stephanie blinked in confusion. "Dares?" she asked, not sure what Jenni meant. She looked at Darcy, but her friend seemed clueless too.

"That's right," Diana answered. "We've come up with three dares for each of you to complete—nothing too major—and once you've done them, your initiation into the club is final. You'll both be full-fledged members of the Flamingoes!"

Darcy was still smiling, but Stephanie was beginning to feel scared. What sort of dares? she wondered. She'd been nervous before, but now she began to feel pretty uncomfortable. And to top it off, her palms had become incredibly sweaty.

Jenni stood up. "There's one other thing," she said, her voice taking on a more serious tone. "You cannot discuss your dares with anyone at all—even with each other. If we find out that you've told anybody about your dares—even another Flamingo—you'll be automatically disqualified. Everything must be kept totally top secret and confidential!"

Darcy looked as if she was raring to go. "When do we get our dares?" she asked enthusiastically.

Jenni smiled. "You'll get your first dare right now. Darcy, you stay here with Diana to hear yours, and Stephanie, you come with me."

Stephanie bit her bottom lip. Standing, she wiped her palms on her jean skirt and followed Jenni into another bedroom—probably Jenni's older sister Susan's bedroom, she thought. Suddenly Stephanie remembered what D.J. had said about Susan Morris. She looked around Susan's bedroom, but she didn't notice anything weird or bad. In fact, Susan's bedroom looked just like D.J.'s! *Oh, what does D.J. know?* Stephanie thought angrily. *She must have said all those bad things about Susan because she's jealous of her.* Stephanie smiled slyly—if only D.J. could see her now!

"Okay, Stephanie," Jenni whispered when they were seated on Susan's bed. "Here's your first dare. Tomorrow evening you have to call Mr. Thomas's house."

Stephanie's eyes widened. "The principal?" she asked, her voice quavering slightly.

"Yes," Jenni replied. "You'll just tell him that you're taking a survey and that you need to ask him a few questions about his job. See how long you can keep him on the phone. It'll be a blast!"

Stephanie felt her palms get sweaty all over again. *How in the world am I going to do this?* she wondered. *Mr. Thomas might know it's me!* She didn't think she could do it. But before she could protest, Jenni went on talking.

"Don't worry," Jenni assured her. "It won't be as hard as you think. It'll be fun. I'll come over around five-thirty and be there to make sure you go through with it."

"To *my* house?" Stephanie asked. This was sounding pretty good! Stephanie had never had an older girl come over before. She could just picture the look on D.J.'s face when Jenni showed up at the Tanners' front door!

Stephanie folded her arms across her chest. She suddenly felt sure that she could do the dare. If it meant that Jenni was coming over . . . she'd just make sure she did it, that was all. "No problem, Jenni," she said confidently. "I'll be waiting."

CHAPTER
5

♦ ◂ ◄ ♦

At lunch the next day Allie didn't ask Stephanie how the Flamingoes meeting went, and Stephanie didn't bring it up. She wanted to tell Allie all about it, but she had promised to keep the meeting a secret—even from Allie. Still, it was hard to sit there and *not* talk about it. Stephanie could hardly think of anything else.

When she got home at four o'clock that afternoon Stephanie flew through the front door and flung her book bag on the sofa. There was so much to be done! Jenni Morris would be coming over in less than two hours, and there wasn't a moment to waste. She bolted to the staircase.

"Hey, Steph, where's the fire?"

Stephanie turned around. She hadn't seen Joey when she came in, but there he was, sitting on the sofa, lifting her book bag off his face and rubbing his nose.

"Oops! Sorry, Joey. I didn't see you." Stephanie went to retrieve her bag.

"That's okay," he said. "But why the rush?"

Stephanie started to tell Joey about Jenni and the Flamingoes but quickly decided against it. If she did, then she'd have to explain why Jenni was coming over in the first place. She couldn't very well see herself saying, "Please excuse us, Joey, but Jenni and I have to go make a prank call to the principal."

"Oh, no big reason," she said. "I've just got a lot of homework to do. A ton."

Joey smiled, but Stephanie thought he looked mildly suspicious. "Well," he said, "it looks as if you just can't wait to get started on it!"

Stephanie decided just to go with his remark as she made her way to the stairs. "That's right!" she exclaimed. "You know how I love doing homework!" And with that, she ran up the steps by twos.

Upstairs, Stephanie tried desperately to make her room look less babyish and more cool. She and D.J. still weren't on good terms, so she couldn't borrow any grown-up things from her. Instead she had to make do with what she had. She started by clearing away all the geeky stuffed animals! Luckily Michelle would never know. She had a play date with one of her friends until dinnertime.

"Good-bye, Mr. Bear," she said as she flung Michelle's stuffed bear into the closet. "See ya later, Froggie Frog and Doggie Dog." For a split second she felt bad tossing Doggie Dog into the closet. Uncle Jesse had won him for her at a fair years ago when he'd first come to live with them. She hated to see that cute little puppy face on the bottom of her closet. Oh, he'll be all right, she figured. It was only for a couple of hours anyway.

Next Stephanie hung up the two posters of Christian Slater that she'd bought from the poster shop on her way home from school. She thumbtacked them up over her bed, then stood back to check them out. *I don't know what the big deal about him is,* she thought. *He can't even wash his hair. But if Jenni thinks Christian Slater is hot—he must be!*

Looking around, Stephanie sighed. There

45

wasn't much else she could do. It wasn't as if she had "instant cool stuff" packed away in a box or anything. She remade her bed, then sat down at her desk to actually do her homework.

When the doorbell rang a little over an hour later, Stephanie almost jumped out of her seat. Jenni was here! She sprang up from her desk and ran to the stairs. *Hold it,* she thought. *I don't want to look too eager.* She took a deep breath to calm herself, checked her hair in the hall mirror, and then started slowly down the stairs.

The doorbell rang again—a long and impatient ring—before Stephanie even got to the bottom of the stairs. She was hurrying toward the door when D.J. cut her off, flying through the living room. "Is that Steve?" D.J. asked hopefully.

Stephanie stopped in her tracks. *Perfect!* she thought. *Wait till D.J. sees who's at the door!* This was even better than she'd imagined.

D.J. pulled open the door. When she saw who stood on the Tanners' front porch, her jaw dropped.

Stephanie was thrilled! She came up behind

D.J. and said as casually as possible, "Jenni, it's so good to see you! Come on in."

Jenni took off her leather jacket as she walked past D.J. and into the house. At the sight of the mirror near the front door, she stopped to fix her hair and check out her tight black jumpsuit. "I was waiting for hours on that porch of yours, Stephanie," she said in a nasty tone. "Can we get started?"

"Get started on what?" asked D.J., who had recovered from her shock and was now looking at Jenni Morris with a mixture of dislike and distrust.

"Yes," said Joey, who had come into the living room without Stephanie noticing. "Get started on what?"

Uh-oh, Stephanie thought. *I'd better get Jenni upstairs fast.*

"On our book reports," Stephanie said quickly. Then, turning to Jenni, she added, "We really ought to get started on those book reports of ours, don't you think? Come on upstairs." Stephanie made a dash for the stairs.

"But, Steph," Joey said. "Aren't you even going to introduce us to your friend?"

Jenni must think this is so lame! Stephanie

47

thought. Clearing her throat, she said, "Oh, right! I'm sorry, Joey. I guess I just had my mind on that book report. Joey, this is Jenni Morris . . . a friend from school. Jenni, this is my dad's college friend, Joey. And this is my sister D.J."

"Hi." Jenni looked totally bored and impatient with the family introductions. "Listen, Stephanie," she said in a loud whisper, "I really don't have time—"

"Right, right," Stephanie said quickly. "Uh, Jenni and I are going upstairs now. C'mon, Jenni."

As the two girls went up the stairs Stephanie heard Joey say, "Not exactly the friendly type, is she?"

She hoped that Jenni couldn't hear D.J.'s answer: "You don't know the half of it."

Up in Stephanie's room, Jenni plopped herself down on Stephanie's bed, looking completely bored. Her arms folded across her chest, she sat with her legs crossed, her top leg bouncing impatiently. Stephanie began trying desperately to entertain her.

"Check this out, Jenni," she said, holding

up a picture of herself taken with the Beach Boys.

Jenni's eyes flicked over the picture, but her bored expression never changed.

"The Beach Boys came over to our house," Stephanie rattled on. "This very house. See this one? He's an old friend of my uncle Jesse's, and Jesse asked them to be on my dad's TV show for a benefit—"

"The Beach Boys are, like, so . . . old," Jenni said. "But who's the hunk?" She pointed to a figure standing beside the band in the picture.

"That's my uncle Jesse," Stephanie said proudly.

Jenni sighed. "Wow. I haven't seen anyone that hot since Mickey moved away. Think you could introduce me?"

Stephanie laughed. "Uncle Jesse's old," she said as if Jenni were crazy. "And anyway, he's married and has twins."

Jenni's face fell. "Oh. Well, anyway, where's the phone? Let's get going."

Stephanie really wasn't looking forward to pranking Mr. Thomas. She needed a bit more time to get herself ready to make her call.

"Oh, right," she mumbled, "the phone."

Then she thought of something. "Hey, wait a sec! I want to show you my new boots." Stephanie ran over to her closet. She cracked it open, hoping that none of Michelle's stuffed animals would come rolling out the door, and pulled out a pair of red cowboy boots that her father had gotten her for her birthday last month. She hadn't even worn them yet. Now she held up the boots for Jenni to admire.

"I'm waiting until I get the perfect outfit to wear them," Stephanie said. "Aren't they cool?"

"They're all right," Jenni said, yawning. "But Doc Martens are in now. Cowboy boots were last year."

Stephanie's heart sank. "Right," she said, tossing the boots carelessly back into the closet. "That's why I'm getting Doctor Martens next weekend."

"*Doc* Martens," Jenni corrected.

"That's what I said," Stephanie said nervously. "Doc Martens. I knew that."

Jenni stood up and walked over to the mirror to check herself out. "Stephanie," she said, "are you going to make this call or what? I thought you wanted to be in the Flamingoes."

"Oh, definitely!" Stephanie reassured her. "I do. Let's go do it right now."

Just then, there was a knock at Stephanie's door.

"Oh, great. Now what?" Stephanie said, secretly happy about the interruption. "Come in!"

The door opened, and D.J. and Steve came in.

Jenni took one look at Steve in the mirror and immediately started tossing her hair around. Turning from the mirror, she walked over and smiled up at him. "Hi there!" she cooed. "I'm Jenni."

"Uh . . . hi. I'm Steve," Steve replied, a bit uncomfortably.

"So what's up?" Stephanie asked, shooting a snotty look at her sister. "Actually, we're pretty busy right now."

"Yeah, you look real busy," D.J. said, staring at her sister and then at Jenni, who had moved even closer to Steve. "I just came in to tell you that Dad called—"

"Hey, I know you," Jenni interrupted, smiling up at Steve and moving closer to him. "Don't you go to school with my sister, Susan Morris? Your name is Steve, right? My sister had the biggest crush on you!" She twirled her long brown hair around her finger and smiled at him.

Stephanie couldn't believe her eyes. Jenni was flirting with Steve—and right under D.J.'s nose!

"Huh?" Steve looked confused. "Oh, wait a minute," he said a second later. "Yeah! Susan Morris! I remember her. I thought you looked familiar," he told Jenni. "Boy, you look a lot like Susan."

Jenni giggled. "Really?" she asked. "No one's ever told me that before. Is that good or bad?"

"Oh, it's good," Steve assured her. "Susan Morris," he repeated. "So what's she been up to these days? Hey, Deej, do you know Susan Morris? She must be in some of your classes. Don't you think Jenni and Susan look a lot alike?"

Stephanie thought she had never seen her sister with the expression that she had on her face right at that moment.

D.J.'s eyes were narrowed, and she spoke through gritted teeth. "Yes, Steve," she said. "She looks just like Susan. They're practically identical twins. Come on now, we have to go."

She took his arm and yanked him toward the door.

"Uh, D.J.?" Stephanie asked, secretly enjoying watching her sister suffer. "Was that his whole message?"

"Whose message?" D.J. asked, annoyed.

"Dad's!" Stephanie replied. Boy, her sister was obviously so distracted by Jenni's flirting, she'd forgotten why she'd come into the room in the first place!

"Oh, right," D.J. said. "Yeah, just that he won't be home until seven, so we'll be eating later."

Stephanie couldn't believe that was the real reason D.J. had barged into her room. After all, their father often came home late from the studio, and it was never a big deal. *She probably just wanted to see what Jenni and I were up to,* Stephanie thought. *She probably never thought I'd be hanging around with such a popular eighth grader.*

"Okay, so he won't be home until seven," Stephanie said sarcastically. "I'll alert the news media."

D.J. gave her sister a dirty look, then pulled Steve out the door.

As the door closed, Jenni smiled over at Stephanie. "Steve's hot," she said. "Are he and your sister, like, a thing?"

Stephanie was impressed that Jenni thought she would even have a chance with a guy who was so much older. She nodded. "They've been going out for more than a year."

"That's too bad," Jenni said, with obvious disappointment. "Though that's never stopped me before!" she added with a laugh.

Stephanie smiled and nodded in agreement, wondering if Jenni meant that she made it a habit of stealing other people's boyfriends.

"So anyway," Jenni said, "it's about time for that phone call."

Stephanie knew she couldn't stall any longer. It was time to make the call and complete her first dare. "Okay," she said slowly. "I'll show you where there's another phone extension." She led Jenni into her father's study and pointed to the phone.

"You can listen in on that line," she said.

Stephanie made sure that the coast was clear and then tiptoed over to her father's bedroom. As she passed her sister's room, even with the door closed she could hear

D.J. and Steve arguing. *Ha!* she thought. *It serves her right!*

Stephanie sat down on her father's bed and stared at the phone. Her hands were shaking a lot, but she was excited just the same. Briefly she wondered whether Darcy's dare was the same as hers. But it didn't really matter. After the call, her first dare would be complete! Then there would be only two more dares left.

She took a deep breath and dialed Mr. Thomas's home phone number, which she'd gotten from the phone book. She'd been up the night before practicing the fake voice she was going to use for the call. It was far lower than her own voice, and she thought it was more mature-sounding. Michelle had heard her practicing and had told her that she was going nuts, but she did admit that Stephanie sounded older.

Stephanie cleared her throat when she heard the phone ring on the other end. Then she heard Jenni pick up the extension. Stephanie crossed her fingers, hoping that Mr. Thomas wouldn't recognize her voice. She didn't want to even think about what would happen if he

55

did. The words *detention* and *grounded for life* came to mind.

"Hello?" a man's deep voice said.

"Uh . . . yes . . . Good evening," Stephanie said. She hoped that her voice wasn't shaking too much. "May I please speak to a Mr. Dwayne Thomas? This is Gloria from Career Surveys, and I would like to ask Mr. Thomas a few questions."

Mr. Thomas seemed hesitant, but at last he replied, "This is Dwayne Thomas. How may I help you?"

Stephanie's heart was racing. Maybe this wasn't going to be so hard after all!

"Mr. Thomas," she said, her confidence building as she spoke, "I understand that you are a junior high school principal."

"Yes, that's correct," he answered.

Stephanie hesitated a second. She hadn't really thought much past this part. Actually, she'd thought Mr. Thomas would have hung up on her by now. She hadn't planned what to say next!

"A junior high school principal," she repeated slowly, as if she were writing it down. "Very good. That's very good."

There was an uncomfortable silence, then Stephanie said, "Uh, Mr. Thomas . . . " Whoops! She was using her normal voice! Clearing her throat, she repeated, "Uh, Mr. Thomas, now how many years have you been a junior high school principal?"

"Sixteen years," he answered slowly. Stephanie thought he sounded a little suspicious.

Then there was another long pause while she desperately tried to think of another question.

"Very good," she said, stalling again. "And, uh, when you were a little boy, did you hope to grow up to become a junior high school principal?"

Mr. Thomas was definitely on to her now. "Excuse me, miss," he said, "but where did you say you were from again?"

Stephanie panicked. She couldn't remember what she'd told him! She couldn't even remember the phony name she'd used!

"Um . . . I'm, um, taking a survey," was all she managed to spit out. "I . . . um . . . need to ask you—"

"That's quite enough," Mr. Thomas said in an angry voice. "You should be ashamed of yourself for bothering people during dinnertime with these childish pranks. I have a good mind to call the—"

Stephanie slammed down the phone and sat on the edge of her father's bed in shock. *I can't believe I did that!* she thought. *What if he recognized my voice?*

Just then, Jenni came into the room. She was all smiles.

"Nice work, Tanner!" she said. She seemed really impressed. "You had him on the phone longer than anyone else!"

Did that mean Darcy had to call Mr. Thomas too? Stephanie wondered. She couldn't believe she had actually gone through with her dare of calling Mr. Thomas. Her mind was still racing. She couldn't remember a word of the conversation. She'd really thought she'd messed it up, but evidently Jenni thought she'd been okay.

Stephanie began to relax. "Oh, that was nothing," she said, smiling back at her Flamingo big sister. "That was a cinch! It was too easy. Maybe I should call him back?"

Jenni laughed. "No, that's not necessary. Your first dare is history. Only two more to go!"

Stephanie felt a rush of excitement. This was going to be easier than she'd thought.

"So what's next?" she asked, ready to take on any dare the Flamingoes had to offer. "You want me to prank the superintendent? The president of the PTA? The school nurse?"

"No, nothing like that. You'll find out your next dare tomorrow," Jenni said mysteriously. "As for now, I'm outta here."

"Oh, you're leaving so soon?" Stephanie was disappointed. She'd been hoping to parade the popular eighth grader around D.J. a few more times. "Can't you hang out awhile longer? My dad will be home soon. You can stay for dinner."

Jenni looked bored at the offer. "That's so cute of you to ask," she said flatly, "but I gotta go meet somebody. Like, where's my jacket?"

Stephanie led Jenni downstairs and retrieved her leather jacket from the closet. Handing it over, she noticed the pink ribbon sewn to the tag inside. *How totally cool!* she thought. Stephanie thought she might be brave enough to wear something pink to school tomorrow. On the other hand, she felt sort of superstitious about it. Probably she

59

should wait until she was a full-fledged Flamingo before she put on any pink.

"Catch ya later, Tanner," Jenni said. And without another word, she walked out the door.

Even though things had gone better than she had dreamed they would, as she watched Jenni Morris walk down the steps in front of her house, Stephanie felt somehow dissatisfied. "Yeah," she replied. "Catch ya later."

CHAPTER
6

♦ ◀ ♦ ♦

The next day at lunch period Stephanie sat with Allie and Darcy. She had so much on her mind, such as the fact that she hadn't heard a word from Jenni about her next dare, that it took her a while to notice that things were unusually quiet at the table.

Darcy was picking at her pizza slice, barely saying a word. She only looked up anxiously when Stephanie started talking about Jenni's visit the evening before. "And when D.J. and Steve came in," Stephanie said, "Jenni started talking to Steve, and I think she was even flirting with him! D.J. was pretty upset. Jenni said—"

"Stephanie," Allie said impatiently, "can we please talk about something other than Jenni Morris? All day long it's been 'Jenni said this' and 'Jenni said that.' I'm really getting tired of hearing about Jenni Morris!"

Stephanie bit her lip. She probably shouldn't have been talking about Jenni and the Flamingoes at all. And especially not when she knew how upset Allie felt. Why had she done that? "I'm sorry, Al," she said sincerely.

Allie stood up and gathered her things. "Never mind," she said. "I have to go talk to Ms. Burns about the play." She looked at Stephanie. "So I'll see you after school at my house?"

Stephanie darted a quick glance at Darcy. They both knew that they would probably have dares to do that afternoon after school. Stephanie hadn't wanted to make any plans, just in case. She looked back at Allie, not knowing what to say.

"After school?" she asked, pretending to be confused.

"Yeah, after school," Allie repeated, her eyes

narrowing. "Don't you remember? We made plans to watch the soaps together. I taped five episodes of 'Day In and Day Out.' "

"Oh, boy! Yes, of course I remember," Stephanie began, "it's just that . . ."

"It's just that you'd rather be with Jenni Morris, right?" Allie said in a huff. "Never mind, Stephanie. I'll see you tomorrow." Angrily she grabbed her sweater, picked up her tray, and stomped out of the cafeteria.

Stephanie put her head down on the table. She felt terrible. She really hadn't meant to hurt Allie's feelings. Why in the world had she gone on and on about Jenni Morris? *Sometimes,* Stephanie thought, *I wish I could keep my big mouth shut!*

Stephanie sighed heavily. She couldn't wait for this initiation to be over. "I just hope," she said, "that when we get to be Flamingoes, we can work on getting Allie in too."

"Yeah," Darcy said. "So how'd your dare go?"

"Oh, fine," Stephanie replied, smoothing out a crease from her T-shirt. "It went great! What about yours?"

"Great," Darcy said, smiling. "It was, like,

fun even! I just didn't want to say anything in front of Allie."

"I shouldn't have either," Stephanie groaned. "I can't believe I went on and on about the Flamingoes and Jenni Morris coming over right in front of her. I feel awful!"

"I just wish she was in on this with us," Darcy said. "Well, anyway, the initiation stage will be over soon. In fact, I have to do my second dare tonight."

Stephanie was envious. She wished she and Darcy could talk about their dares. Why had Darcy heard about hers already when Stephanie hadn't? She was dying to ask Darcy what her first dare had been, but she didn't want to break the Flamingoes' sacred "code of silence" that Jenni had warned her about.

Darcy seemed uneasy talking about the dares, too. "Was, um, your first dare, like, hard or something?"

Stephanie didn't know what to say. She knew what she'd *like* to say—she'd like to tell Darcy everything! She'd been up half the night worrying about whether or not Mr. Thomas had recognized her voice. She wondered if Darcy'd had to make a prank call to him too.

"No, it wasn't too hard," she told Darcy at last. "It was just, I don't know, just a dare." Both girls were silent for a minute.

"This is going to be really great, Stephanie," Darcy finally said. "I'm so glad we're both going to be Flamingoes!"

"Me too," Stephanie said. "I just wish Allie had been asked. It doesn't feel right without her." She was thoughtful for a moment and then went on. "Anyway, I have to get going. I want to try and catch up with her and, you know, apologize again."

"Okay, Steph," Darcy said. "I guess I'll *catch ya later!*"

Stephanie laughed at Darcy's attempt to sound like Jenni Morris. Then she picked up her book bag and left the cafeteria, heading for Allie's locker.

Walking through the halls, she began to think about the whole dare situation. Why had she and Darcy been sworn to secrecy in the first place? What was the big deal in talking about her dares with Darcy? But what troubled her most was that Darcy had already heard about her next dare. She hadn't heard a thing!

65

On her way past the principal's office, Stephanie put her head down and walked quickly, staring at the floor. She hoped that nobody would recognize her. Especially not Mr. Thomas!

Stephanie was just down the hall from Allie's locker when she heard someone call out her name. Turning her head, she saw Diana Rink and two of her friends—both Flamingoes—waving. Instinctively she turned and looked behind her to see who they were waving to. But the hallway was empty.

"Oh!" said Stephanie, surprised. Then she put up a hand and waved back. As the three girls walked over to her, a bell rang, and the hall began to fill up with kids changing classes. Out of the corner of her eye Stephanie saw Allie at her locker. She'd wanted to talk to Allie, but now the timing was all wrong. She didn't want Allie to see her talking to Diana, either. The last thing she wanted to do was rub her friendship with the Flamingoes in Allie's face.

"Hi!" Stephanie said, checking out Diana's awesome outfit. She was decked out in pink, except for her big, black, clunky shoes. Stephanie noted that although Diana was pretty and had

66

great clothes, she went a little overboard on the eye makeup.

"Hi, Stephanie!" Diana said in a friendly voice.

"Hi, Stephanie," the two Flamingoes with her echoed.

"Excellent work on your first dare, Tanner," said Diana. "You are definitely proving yourself worthy of becoming a Flamingo."

Stephanie beamed. She secretly hoped that people were watching—and noticing that she was a big buddy of Diana and her friends. She also secretly hoped that at this very moment Allie wasn't watching.

"Those are really cool Doc Martens," Stephanie said, making sure to call the shoes "Doc Martens" and not "Doctor Martens."

Diana smiled proudly. "Thanks. I bought them at the mall yesterday. They cost a small fortune, but they're so bad! Anyway," she continued, "you might want to be home today around four or so to get a, you know, phone call from a Flamingo." Diana let her voice trail off mysteriously.

"Ah," said Stephanie. "Ah . . . right, I think I get your message, and for sure I'll be there."

67

Just then, Brandon Fallow walked down the hall. He was wearing a plaid work shirt tied around his waist, jeans, and work boots. He looked so cool. Stephanie froze.

"Hey, Diana," Brandon said.

"Hi, Brandon," Diana said.

"Hi, Brandon!" said the two other Flamingoes.

Stephanie was too nervous to say anything. She watched him stroll easily down the hallway and turn a corner. She had never felt so happy. Brandon Fallow had seen her—*her*—talking to the Flamingoes. He must have noticed her. Maybe next time he would actually say hi to her!

"So we have to go now," Diana said, nodding to her friends. "Good luck with dare number two. Catch ya later, Tanner."

"Catch ya later," the other Flamingoes echoed.

Stephanie watched as the trio of pink disappeared down the hall. She took a deep breath to calm herself down, and then she walked slowly over to Allie's locker. Was it her imagination, or were all eyes watching her as she walked down the hallway? So this was what it felt like to be in with the cool crowd! To be the envy of every sixth-grade girl in the hall. Fantastic!

But as she drew closer to Allie's locker, Stephanie's mood changed. She really did feel bad about what she had done at lunch. *If only Allie had been asked to join the Flamingoes too,* Stephanie thought. *Then everything wouldn't be so . . . complicated.*

Allie was just closing her locker when Stephanie got there.

"Allie," Stephanie began, "listen, I'm really, really sorry about the way I acted at lunch."

Allie shrugged. "That's okay," she said. "I know you're just excited about the Flamingoes and everything. I see you're getting pretty chummy with Diana Rink, too."

Stephanie bit her lip. She didn't know what to say. Obviously Allie had seen her talking with the Flamingoes in the hall. She was so tempted to explain everything—to tell Allie about the dares and that she shouldn't worry about not being asked to join because as soon as she'd been made a Flamingo, she'd get Allie in too.

"Oh, Diana is no big deal," Stephanie said,

69

trying to sound as if she meant it. "Listen, Allie, do you want me to not try out for the Flamingoes? I mean, if it's going to come between us, then I can just tell Jenni and Diana to forget the whole thing."

Stephanie held her breath. She wanted to be a Flamingo more than anything. But she would give it all up for Allie's sake, if that's what her best friend really, *really* wanted. But of course, she hoped Allie didn't!

Allie stared back at Stephanie. "You'd really give up being a Flamingo for me?"

"Well, of course," Stephanie answered, hoping she sounded convincing. "But," she added, "I have another idea."

"What's that?" Allie asked.

"Well," Stephanie said, "if I get into the Flamingoes, I could talk to Jenni and get you in too. And if they wouldn't let you in, then I'd quit."

Allie looked sad. "Stephanie," she said, "you don't really want to forget about becoming a Flamingo, do you?"

"No," Stephanie admitted. "But I will if you want . . ."

"No, no, no. I don't," Allie said. "Listen, just

because you were asked and I wasn't doesn't mean you shouldn't try out."

"Do you mean that?" Stephanie asked.

"Yes."

"Allie, you're the best friend in the world," Stephanie told her sincerely. "I mean it! But I'm still going to try to get you in too. I promise!"

"Okay," Allie said finally. "That sounds like a good plan."

"Great!" Stephanie was glad they had cleared things up. The last thing she wanted was to lose Allie's friendship. "So," she said, "what do you want to do this weekend?"

"I don't know." Allie shrugged. "What do you want to do?"

"I don't know. Maybe we could go to the mall and look at Doc Martens," Stephanie suggested.

"Doc Martens? But you just got cowboy boots from your dad," Allie reminded her.

"Oh, Allie," Stephanie said, "cowboy boots are so last year."

"Huh?" Allie looked at Stephanie as if she were from another planet. "C'mon, let's walk to class together."

The two girls were making their way down the hall, quietly discussing Adam Green and Brandon Fallow and their own possible plans for the weekend, when Stephanie realized that for a few minutes she'd forgotten all about what Diana Rink had told her. Tonight she'd be getting a phone call from a Flamingo. Tonight she'd be finding out about her second dare.

"Steph?" Allie said. "Have you heard one word I've been saying?"

"Of course!" Stephanie reassured her.

Allie looked a little suspicious as they stopped in front of her classroom. "Well, here's where I get off," she said. "I'll call you later?"

"Definitely," Stephanie said, and then added, "Uh, make it after four, okay?"

Allie nodded.

"And, Allie," she added, "I really am sorry about before, at lunch. Sometimes I have a really big mouth! I'm glad you're not mad."

Allie grinned. "How could I ever be mad at my very best friend?"

The bell rang, and once again Stephanie was going to be late for class. She made a face, then smiled at Allie. "I'll talk to you later!" Then she ran down the hall, feeling happy that things were patched up between her and Allie. Allie was the most understanding friend ever. Boy— she had a true friend, plus she was on her way to becoming a Flamingo! How lucky could one girl get?

Sure enough, at four o'clock sharp, the phone rang at the Tanner house. Stephanie picked it up, wondering what was in store for her. She hoped her second dare was going to go as smoothly as the first one had.

"Hello?" Stephanie said.

"Hello, Tanner," came Diana's voice from the phone. "Ready for dare number two?"

"Ready," Stephanie replied.

"Okay, here it is. For your next dare, you must call up Allie Taylor."

"Allie?" Stephanie said hopefully. Maybe she herself would be the one who would tell Allie that she could try out for the Flamingoes!

"That's right. Say you're from *Sassy* magazine and tell Allie that she'll win a free makeover if she tells you the name of the boy she has a secret crush on."

"What?" Stephanie couldn't believe her ears.

"I'll be over around eight tonight to listen in on the call. Catch ya later!" *Click.*

Stephanie felt as if she'd had the wind knocked out of her. Slowly she put the receiver back in its cradle. Make a prank call to Allie? How could she possibly prank Allie? It wasn't right. She couldn't do something so terrible to her best friend. Plus, what if she did the dare and Allie actually fell for the story about *Sassy* and talked about her crush on Adam? Diana would be there listening on the other extension. Allie would be totally humiliated if she ever found out!

That settled it. When Diana came over that night, Stephanie would just tell her right out that she couldn't possibly do the dare. The Flamingoes would have to come up with some other dare for her to do, and that was that.

Suddenly Stephanie felt a little better. After all, Diana had been so nice to her in the hallway before. Surely she would understand that Stephanie could never do anything so mean.

"What's the matter, Stephanie?" asked Michelle, who had just come into the living room.

"You look like you're working on a big fat math problem inside your head."

"Ohhh, Michelle," Stephanie moaned. "That's exactly how I feel."

But everything will work out, Stephanie told herself. *It just has to!*

CHAPTER
7

♦ ◄ ◗ ♦

"I don't understand what the problem is." Diana sat with her feet up on Stephanie's bed. She hadn't even bothered to take off her Doc Martens. Stephanie didn't think she was acting friendly at all. In fact, Diana looked bored and annoyed.

Stephanie sighed. This conversation was not going the way she'd planned. Stephanie plopped down next to Diana and started to explain again. "I told you," she said. "Allie is my best friend. Why would you even want me in your club if I was so rotten to my very best friend? It doesn't make sense. Just give me another dare to do . . . anything! Anything that doesn't involve Allie."

Diana shook her head. "I don't know, Stephanie," she said. "We thought you had more guts than this. We all thought for sure that you'd be the one to complete all the dares. Now it looks as if only Darcy will become a Flamingo."

Stephanie was crushed. "Okay, wait a sec," she said, desperately trying to think of something. "What if I just make the call, but ask Allie something else? Something not about guys."

Diana was growing impatient. "Stephanie, the dare has to be done exactly the way the Flamingoes created it. I can't change it. What's the big deal, anyway? The dare is only to see if you have the guts to become a Flamingo. After the initiation, you can call up Allie and tell her that it was all just a joke. You two will have a few good laughs over it."

Stephanie knew that Diana was wrong. Allie wouldn't think that this prank was funny, ever. She looked sideways at Diana, who was thumbing impatiently through a magazine. Stephanie wondered if the girl sitting here in her bedroom was really the friendly Flamingo she'd spoken to today in the hallway.

Suddenly the bedroom door flew open. In

walked Michelle and two of her friends from school. They had finger paints all over their faces and were singing some horrible song at the top of their voices about a genie who came out of a magic bottle. Stephanie was mortified.

"Michelle!" she yelled. "What do you think you're doing? I told you—we need privacy!"

"Yes, I know," Michelle said innocently. She turned to her friends and put a finger to her lips. "Shhh! Let's be quiet so they can have privacy."

"Oh, for heaven's sake!" Diana made a face. "Stephanie, I think we ought to just forget the whole thing."

"No! Wait!" Stephanie pleaded. "Michelle and her friends are just leaving—*right*, Michelle?" She looked meaningfully at her little sister.

"But this is my room too," Michelle protested. "And we want privacy too."

Now Michelle's friends began to chant, "We want privacy! We want privacy!"

Stephanie felt her face turning red. She wished she could stuff Michelle and her friends into a magic bottle! Instead, she turned to bribery.

"Michelle," Stephanie said in her sweetest, most sisterly voice. "If you and your friends will leave us alone, I promise to make brownies for you when we're through up here."

The kids stopped their chanting and looked at Stephanie.

"Double fudge with chocolate icing?" Michelle asked.

Life can't get much more embarrassing than this, Stephanie thought. "Yes," she replied weakly, "double fudge with chocolate icing."

"And you'll play Barbies with us?" Michelle asked.

"Yes! Yes! Anything!" Stephanie pleaded. "Just get out."

Michelle and her friends marched out of the room, chanting, "Brownies and Barbie! Brownies and Barbie!"

Stephanie slammed the door behind them and leaned against it. "Sorry about that, Diana," she said meekly. "Um, where were we?"

Diana stood. "We were discussing the dare. Are you going to do it or not?"

Stephanie had to make a decision. She knew Diana was growing very impatient.

"I . . . I . . ." Stephanie didn't know *what* she was going to say.

Just then, Diana reached into her book bag and pulled out an awesome pink-and-lavender friendship bracelet.

"Oh," she said. "I totally forgot to show this to you! This is the new Flamingoes friendship bracelet we had made for you—isn't it excellent? I was hoping you'd be able to wear it." She laid the bracelet on Stephanie's bed. "Why don't you put it on now, just while you make the phone call?"

Stephanie's eyes widened. "Wow! It's great!" she gushed, picking it up and trying it on. *I must have this bracelet,* she thought desperately. *Allie will just have to understand that it was a joke, that's all.*

Clenching her teeth, Stephanie said, "Okay, let's do it."

"Fine," Diana said. "And here." From her purse she pulled out a scarf and handed it to Stephanie. "Wrap this over the receiver and disguise your voice. Allie will never know it's you."

Stephanie took the handkerchief and led the way out into the hallway. She was about to show Diana in to her father's study, where she could listen in on his phone extension, when she nearly bumped into D.J. When D.J. saw Diana, her eyes widened. Stephanie knew she was surprised to see *another* eighth grader here with her.

"What are you doing, Stephanie?" D.J. asked.

"Do you mind?" Stephanie asked. "We would like some privacy."

"Fine with me," D.J. replied. She turned quickly and walked into her room, closing her door with a thud. Stephanie heard her lock it behind her.

Stephanie showed Diana the phone in her father's study and then went to her father's bedroom to make the call from the phone in there. She sat for a full minute on her dad's bed before picking up the phone. *Allie will forgive me,* she tried to reason with herself as she wrapped the handkerchief around the bottom half of the receiver. *She'll understand that I simply had to do this! When it's all over and we're both Flamingoes, we'll laugh about the whole thing.*

Stephanie prayed silently that Allie wouldn't fall for the prank. She hoped she wouldn't reveal anything too private—especially anything about Adam Green! Not with Diana listening in. Taking a deep breath, Stephanie crossed the fingers of one hand and began dialing with the other.

After four rings, Stephanie breathed a sigh of relief—Allie wasn't home! But just as she was about to hang up, the ringing stopped.

"Hello?" Allie said.

Oh, no! Stephanie didn't know what to say. Maybe she should just hang up, but Diana was listening in.

"Hello?" Allie said again.

Stephanie cleared her throat. "Uh, yes, hello," she croaked in a deep voice, hoping she didn't sound anything like herself. "Yes, may I speak with Alison Taylor, please?"

Allie hesitated for a moment, then answered. "This is Allie Taylor," she said, a bit suspiciously. "Who is this?"

"Congratulations, Allie," Stephanie said quickly, her mind spinning, trying to remember just what Diana had told her to say. And suddenly she had an idea! Somehow she'd give away that this was a prank call, and Allie would hang up before she had a chance to ask the personal questions. Perfect! The Flamingoes would just have to count her dare as complete, and Allie wouldn't have revealed any secrets about Adam.

"My name is Tabitha," Stephanie said, "and I'm a writer for *Sassy* magazine."

"A writer from *Sassy*?" Allie asked in disbelief.

Remembering to keep her voice as deep and crackly as possible, Stephanie went on. "Yes. Um, we've selected your name from our list of subscribers," she said, "and I'm happy to tell you that you've won a free makeover." Stephanie noticed that her voice was crackling and shaking. She was so scared! *Please, Allie*, she thought, *don't fall for this! Hang up now!*

"A makeover?" Allie asked shyly. "Wow, I've never won anything like this before."

"Um, yes," Stephanie continued, stalling for time and hoping Allie would get wise and hang up, "a free makeover."

"I don't remember entering a contest or anything. How could I have won a makeover?"

"This wasn't a contest," Stephanie said. "We just picked your name. We'll mail you a certificate for the makeover, but first you have to answer a few questions."

"Questions about what?"

Allie wasn't hanging up! Stephanie needed a new plan—quick! What if she just asked Allie *other* questions? Nothing at all about Adam. Then, later, she could just tell Diana that she forgot the exact question she was supposed to ask Allie.

"Well," Stephanie said, "questions like this. How old are you?"

"Eleven."

"And what grade are you in?"

"Sixth grade."

This isn't so bad, Stephanie thought. "And where do you live?"

"On Foothill Lane in San Francisco."

"What type of music do you like?"

"Dance music, I guess."

"And . . ." But before Stephanie could ask another question, she looked up and saw Diana standing in the doorway. Her hands were on her hips. She gave Stephanie a mean look and shook her head, as if to say that this phone call wasn't going to count if she didn't get to the big question. Then Diana turned and went back to the study.

Stephanie felt her stomach churn. This whole

thing was making her sick. Diana was making her sick! She wished she had never agreed to call Allie in the first place. But she had, and now she had to go through with it—just the way the Flamingoes wanted—or she could kiss that friendship bracelet good-bye.

"The next question," Stephanie mumbled into the handkerchief, "is about teenage romance."

"Romance?"

"Yes," Stephanie replied. "It's for a story we're working on for the magazine."

"Well, okay. Go ahead, I guess."

"Do you have a crush on any guy in particular?" Stephanie held her breath, hoping again that Allie wouldn't answer.

"A crush?" Allie sounded embarrassed. "Um, no. Uh-uh. No, I mean, sort of, but not really."

All right! Stephanie thought. Allie wasn't going to talk about Adam after all. Whew!

But then Allie giggled shyly and kept talking. "Well, I suppose I could tell you. I mean, you don't even know him. Actually, I have a crush on this really gorgeous football player at school. His name is—"

Stephanie jumped in quickly. "Oh, no . . . that's okay!" she said, cutting Allie off before she could say Adam's name. "You don't have to tell me his name."

"But I wasn't going to tell you his last name." Allie sounded a little confused. "Don't you need to know his first name . . . you know, for your story?"

"No!" Stephanie replied in a panic. "No names! We're just, like, taking a poll, that's all. We're not using any names." *Boy*, thought Stephanie, *this was getting sticky! Since when is Allie so talkative?*

"Oh, okay. Well, anyway, he has these amazing green eyes and he was just made team quarterback."

Stephanie's heart sank. *Oh, Allie!* she thought. *Why did you have to say that?* Now Diana would definitely know she was talking about Adam. Stephanie fell back on her father's bed and covered her eyes with the back of her arm. This was all her fault. How could she possibly have done this?

Meanwhile Allie—who was usually shy when it came to boys—kept right on talking. "He doesn't even know I'm alive. I just follow him around school all day, hoping he'll notice me."

Stephanie couldn't take this anymore. She

was totally humiliating her best friend! She felt like dirt. Worse than dirt. She felt like mud.

"Uh . . . thank you, Miss Taylor," she blurted out. "We'll be in touch with you concerning your free makeover." Then she slammed down the receiver. She was very close to tears.

Suddenly Diana was standing in the doorway again. This time she was grinning from ear to ear. "Good job, Tanner!" she said. "You've definitely got the guts to become a Flamingo!"

At that moment, Stephanie wasn't sure she even wanted to become a Flamingo. Especially if the Flamingoes enjoyed doing such awful things to their friends. She glanced at the friendship bracelet, which was still on her wrist. She had wanted it so badly. Now she couldn't even look at it. She slid it off her arm and handed it back to Diana.

"It'll be yours soon enough," Diana said knowingly. Then she walked back into Stephanie's room and gathered up her things. Stephanie was glad Diana was leaving. She wasn't feeling so good.

"Isn't that cute?" Diana said as she and Stephanie went downstairs. "Allie has a crush on Adam Green. Like he would ever ask her out!

Anyway, take it easy, Stephanie. I'm going over to Jenni's now to report on your second dare. Nice job. Catch ya later."

"Yeah, catch ya later," Stephanie muttered as Diana walked out the front door.

When she was gone, Stephanie ran up to her room and closed her door. She threw herself down on her bed and started to cry. She felt so twisted up inside. She had betrayed her best friend. All for the sake of joining the Flamingoes.

Was it really worth it?

CHAPTER
8

The next morning, Friday, Stephanie was by the pay phone at school, nervously pacing back and forth, chewing on her thumbnail. She'd missed the early bus, so she went to the pay phone to be sure she could talk to Allie. Stephanie had to see if Allie'd suspected the call had been a prank. And if Allie knew it was Stephanie who had made the call.

But at twenty minutes to eight, there was still no sign of Allie. Stephanie watched as the students made their way to their homerooms. *C'mon, Allie*, thought Stephanie. *Where are you?*

Suddenly there was a tap on her shoulder.

"Allie!" Stephanie cried, turning around. But it wasn't Allie.

"Hi, Stephanie," said Jenni Morris, grinning an enormous grin. "I heard about your dare last night. Excellent!"

"Oh, hi, Jenni," Stephanie said. "Thanks, but I really feel pretty awful about that dare and—"

Jenni didn't let her finish. "Stephanie, lighten up. You're doing a great job. Don't worry. Both you and Darcy are proving yourselves to be total Flamingo material. And now there's only one more dare left." She smiled. "Stay by the phone tonight to find out about dare number three."

This time the thought of a phone call from a Flamingo didn't excite Stephanie. "Listen, Jenni, I want to talk to you about Allie." She'd been up half the night thinking about the Flamingoes and her prank call. Though she wanted to be a Flamingo in the worst way, she was having doubts about joining the club. She didn't think being in the Flamingoes was worth stabbing your best friend in the back!

Just then, out of the corner of her eye, Stephanie saw Brandon Fallow. And he was walking toward them! She felt her pulse begin to quicken, and her palms got all sweaty. *Oh, wow,* she thought. *I hope he comes over! I hope he comes over!*

Then, to Stephanie's amazement, Jenni called out to him. "Hi, Brandon! How are you?"

Brandon flashed them a smile and came right over. Stephanie thought she would die! He was standing less than a foot away from her, and she could see him up close and personal. She leaned on a locker for support, sure her weak knees would give out at any moment.

"I'm fine," Brandon said, flashing an awesome smile that made Stephanie melt. "What's up?"

Stephanie was glad that Jenni could speak, because although she could think of a million things to say to Brandon, she couldn't get a single word out. She just smiled and nodded and listened as Jenni and Brandon talked about tomorrow morning's big soccer game.

"For sure," Jenni said. "We'll be there. Right, Stephanie?"

What was this? Was Jenni asking her to go to the soccer game with her? To see Brandon play? What, was she kidding? Of course she'd be there!

"Oh, yeah, for sure," was all Stephanie could say.

"Great," Brandon said, smiling right at her.

"Well, I gotta go. I've got gym first period, and I need to warm up. Catch ya later!"

Stephanie held her breath and watched him go into the gym. As soon as he was out of sight, she exhaled and turned to Jenni. She knew her face was flushed and probably pinker than a Flamingo's pinkie nail. "Are . . . are you pretty good friends with Brandon?" she asked.

Jenni smiled smugly. "Sure. Brandon and I are, like, really good friends." She paused and added, "Don't you know him? I'm sorry. I'll introduce you to him after the game tomorrow."

Stephanie could hardly contain her excitement. This changed everything! She just had to become a Flamingo. If it meant hanging around with Brandon Fallow and going to his soccer games, she'd do whatever it took. Allie would understand.

"Anyway, Stephanie, I'll talk to you tonight about your last dare," Jenni said. "Darcy'll get her last dare too, and I guess you'll both be sworn in pretty soon."

Then Jenni spotted some of her friends down the hall. "Catch ya later!" she said. In a flash of pink, she was gone.

"Yeah," Stephanie said dreamily. "Later!"

Stephanie was still in a fog. All she could think about was watching Brandon play soccer. Why, he was practically her friend already. Hadn't he smiled directly at her? She couldn't wait to tell Allie!

Stephanie looked at her watch. It was eight minutes to eight, and there was still no sign of Allie. She decided to walk over to her locker. Maybe Allie was waiting for her there.

As Stephanie rounded a corner in the hallway, she saw that she'd been right. Allie was waiting for Stephanie at her locker. Her eyes were darting anxiously from person to person. And when she spotted Stephanie, a huge smile broke across her face and she frantically waved her over.

Whew, Stephanie thought. *Allie doesn't look angry.*

Stephanie had barely made it to her locker when Allie blurted out, "Guess what!" She was positively beaming.

"I was waiting for you at the phone," Stephanie said.

"Oh! Sorry about that. I had to come in early this morning to hand in an extra-credit assignment. I thought I'd miss you at the phone. But forget about that. Guess what happened to me!"

"What?" Stephanie asked, though she had a strange feeling she knew what Allie was about to say.

"I got a call from a writer at *Sassy* yesterday! I won a free makeover! Can you believe it?"

Stephanie tried to act surprised. "Wow! Really?"

"Yes! It was so cool. They got my name from some subscription list or something, and they asked me a bunch of questions about—"

"That's really great," Stephanie interrupted. Her stomach was doing flips again. She really didn't want to hear any more or be reminded of the awful thing she had done. "Listen, Allie, I gotta run to class. Uh, tell me all about it at lunch, okay?"

Allie seemed a bit disappointed, but she had to get to her first-period class too. "Oh, okay, Steph," she said, and then she called after her, "Hey, Steph! You'll come with me to the makeover, right?"

"Definitely!" Stephanie yelled over her shoulder. "For sure!"

Stephanie barely made it to class before the bell rang.

"Ah, Miss Tanner. Glad to see you before the

bell for a change," Mr. Machlin said as Stephanie took her seat in science.

Stephanie smiled and tried to look as if she were paying attention. But right now, she had more important things to think about . . . like what she was going to wear to the soccer game tomorrow.

By lunchtime Stephanie had decided that she'd wear her black jeans to the game. She liked the way she looked in them. The only problem was, she didn't have a cool top that would match. D.J. had a lot of cool tops. But she and D.J. still weren't friendly. There was no way D.J. would let her borrow any of her clothes.

As she walked into the cafeteria, Stephanie had just begun to plot how she could get D.J. to lend her a top. She saw Allie and Darcy already sitting in their usual spot and slowly made her way to the table. She was not looking forward to hearing about Allie's makeover.

As soon as Stephanie sat down, Allie began babbling away about the call from *Sassy*. Darcy seemed to be interested and asked her a load of questions. Stephanie was glad she didn't have to say anything. She wondered what Darcy's second dare had been.

All of a sudden, Allie stopped speaking right in the middle of a sentence. She turned white as a ghost.

Stephanie spun around in her seat and followed Allie's gaze to—Adam Green! He was on his way over to their table!

Stephanie quickly looked back at Allie to see what she'd do. Adam was definitely coming toward them, and Stephanie thought from the way Allie looked, she might pass out. But before anyone could say or do anything, Adam sat down across from them.

"Hi," he said, grinning.

Allie was completely speechless, so Stephanie returned the greeting. "Hi," she said.

Adam stared at Allie.

"You're Allie Taylor, right?" he asked.

Allie managed to nod. She looked as if she might keel over at any moment. "Uh-huh," she said.

"Hi. I . . . um . . . I heard that you had something to ask me," he said awkwardly.

Allie was dumbfounded. She darted a look at Stephanie.

"Uh, where did you hear that?" Allie asked shyly.

Adam shrugged. "Some of your friends"—he pointed to a table a few rows away—"told me you wanted to talk to me."

Stephanie gulped. Adam was pointing to the Flamingoes' table! There sat Diana and a few other Flamingoes, pointing at Adam and Allie and laughing.

Allie looked utterly confused. "My friends?" she asked, looking over his shoulder.

Stephanie's face began to turn bright red. *I can't believe this!* she thought. Diana actually told Adam what Allie said about him. And obviously she'd told the other girls too. This was terrible! Stephanie knew that she was the only person Allie had ever told about her crush on Adam— aside from Tabitha from *Sassy*. Now what if she put two and two together? *What if she figures out it was me who made the call?*

Allie looked as though she would die of embarrassment. She glanced over to Stephanie to see if Stephanie knew what on earth was going on.

But Stephanie quickly turned away from Allie's eyes, sure that her beet red face would give her away.

Adam sensed that something wasn't right. "You did tell them you had to talk to me, didn't you?" he asked. Then he looked over to Diana and noticed she was laughing. "Oh, I get it," he said. He sounded annoyed. "Diana and her stupid tricks. She and her friends are up to something. I'm gonna go see what kind of game they're playing this time."

When Adam left, Allie jumped up from the table and grabbed her book bag. "I don't know what's going on," she said in a shaky voice. "But I really have to go." With that, she picked up her tray and hurried from the table.

Stephanie saw that her eyes were filled with tears.

CHAPTER
9

◆ ◀ ◀ ◆

"Allie—wait up!" Stephanie yelled, running through the cafeteria after her. People were staring at her, but she didn't care. She had never seen her friend so upset.

"Leave me alone!" Allie cried as she stopped just outside the cafeteria. Tears were streaming down her cheeks. "You told them! You told the Flamingoes about me and Adam! I can't believe I ever trusted you!" Allie ran off.

Stephanie felt worse than she'd ever felt in her life. She knew it was all her fault. Still, why had Diana sent Adam over to their table? Feeling furious, she headed back to the cafeteria to look for Diana. She had to find out for herself why she would do such a lousy, cruel thing.

Back in the cafeteria, Stephanie glanced at the Flamingoes' table and saw that Diana had already left. But Jenni was there. *She must have just gotten to the cafeteria*, Stephanie thought. She didn't remember seeing her there before.

"Hi, Stephanie!" Jenni called out cheerfully. "Come on over and hang out awhile."

Stephanie walked over to the table. "Can I talk to you, Jenni? In private?"

Jenni looked curious. "Sure." She turned to her friends. "I'll be back in a flash."

Stephanie and Jenni moved over to an empty table. "So what's this all about?" Jenni asked.

"It's about the dare I had to do last night."

"Oh, that," Jenni said, smiling. "Diana told us what an awesome job you did. But I already told you that this morning."

"Yeah, I know," Stephanie said. "But there's a problem."

Jenni's eyes narrowed. "A problem?" she asked. "You're not chickening out now, are you?"

"No, no . . . it's nothing like that," Stephanie assured her. "It's just that I think that Diana might have . . ." She took a deep breath, then continued, "Diana might have told Adam Green something that Allie said on the phone last night, and now Allie is, like, totally embarrassed and humiliated and she's not speaking to me. She thinks I'm the one who told."

Jenni looked concerned. "Are you sure, Stephanie? Are you positive that it was Diana who said something to Adam?"

"Well, I'm not one hundred percent positive, but I think it was her."

Jenni shook her head. "Well, I've known Diana a long time," she said. "And I can't believe she would ever do anything like that! But if you want me to find out for you, I will. We Flamingoes always stick together, Stephanie. Don't ever forget that. And don't worry about Allie. I'll talk to her if you want. Actually, we're considering asking Allie to try out for the Flamingoes too. Do you think she'd want to?"

"Sure!" Stephanie exclaimed. "Yes! I'm sure she'd want to join!" This was all going to turn out just fine. Allie was going to be a Flamingo too.

"Great!" Jenni said. "That settles it. I'll talk to Allie after school and clear everything up."

"But what about Diana?" Stephanie asked. "What she did—I mean, if she did it—was awful. She really embarrassed Allie."

Jenni didn't look concerned one bit. "I told you," she said, "I'll handle it. Allie and Diana— everything. Don't worry! Now, as for you—you still have one more dare left, which I'm sure you'll complete with no problem." She smiled at Stephanie. "I knew we were right about asking you to try out," she added. "You're gonna make an awesome Flamingo! Now, I gotta get going, so . . . I'll see ya tomorrow."

"Tomorrow?" Stephanie asked.

"At the soccer game," Jenni reminded her.

"Definitely!" Stephanie said, happy to be reminded of Brandon. "I'll be there."

"Radical," Jenni said, walking back to the Flamingoes' table.

When Jenni was gone, Stephanie leaned back in her chair and put her hands behind her head. Okay, things weren't that bad. In less than twenty-four hours, she'd complete her third dare and be a Flamingo. And Allie would be just getting her three dares. Suddenly all the bad feeling about Allie flooded back. *But it's just temporary*, thought Stephanie. *I just have to put up with her being mad at me for a little while. And then she'll totally forgive me.*

How right she'd been to have that private little talk with Jenni. She'd promised to patch things up with everyone. *This is what the coolest club in school is all about,* thought Stephanie. When things got tough, you could always count on the Flamingoes.

CHAPTER
10

◆ ◀ ◆ ◆

"Why are you sitting on the couch with the phone in your lap?" Michelle asked Stephanie.

"I'm expecting an important call," Stephanie said.

"From a boy?" Michelle asked.

"No, not from a boy."

"From a teacher?"

Stephanie shook her head. "Listen, Michelle, don't you have anything better to do than bug me right now? Don't you want to fill up Comet's water dish or something?"

"No," Michelle said, sitting down beside her

sister on the couch. "I want to help you wait for your phone call."

"Michelle," Stephanie said, her voice dripping with sweetness, "remember how I made brownies for you and your little friends?"

"Uh-huh."

"And remember how much fun we had playing Barbies?"

Michelle nodded.

"Well, if you ever, *ever* want me to make brownies for you or play Barbies with you again, then right now you will let me *have some PRIVACY!*"

Michelle got to her feet in a flash. "Comet!" she called as she walked into the kitchen. "I'm coming to get you some fresh water!"

The minute Michelle left the room, the phone rang.

Stephanie picked it up before the first ring finished. "Hello?"

"Stephanie? It's me, Jenni."

"Hi, Jenni."

"Okay, I've got your last dare. Can you talk? There's no chance anyone's listening in on this conversation, is there?"

"No way!"

"For your last dare, Tanner," Jenni said, "you must get your father's phone credit card and bring it to Diana's house tomorrow morning. Got it?"

"My dad's phone card?" Stephanie repeated, feeling her stomach start to knot up again.

"Oh, but don't, like, worry about the credit card. We're not going to use it or anything. We just want to see if you have the nerve to take it."

"Oh," Stephanie said, feeling relieved to hear this, and relieved that the third dare didn't involve any kind of prank call.

"The Flamingoes are planning a club day at the mall tomorrow after the soccer game, so bring it by Diana's house early, like ten o'clock. Then you can come hang out with us at the game and at the mall."

"Great," Stephanie said.

"Okay, Tanner. Catch ya tomorrow!" And with that, Jenni hung up.

Stephanie put down the phone and breathed a sigh of relief. Even though she wasn't too thrilled with this latest dare, at least she wouldn't be hurting anybody's feelings by doing it. And Jenni said that they wouldn't use the card, so what harm could it do? This third dare was going to be much easier than the first two. Tonight, after dinner, she'd just go into her dad's study and take the calling card out of his top right-hand desk drawer. No sweat! She'd have it back by the end of the day, and he'd never even know it was missing.

Stephanie knocked on the door to her father's study.

"Come in, Stephanie," her dad called.

"How did you know it was me, Dad?" Stephanie said, opening the door.

"Because you've been interrupting me for the past hour and a half, that's how," he said, putting down his pen and shutting off his tape recorder.

"Oh, well, sorry about that," Stephanie said. She hoped her father wasn't becoming too suspicious. "I—I . . . I forgot to get a black felt-tip pen from you the last time I was in here."

Danny eyed her curiously. "Didn't you take a pen with you about the fifth time you came in?"

Stephanie froze. "Did I?"

"Yup," Danny replied. "You did."

"Oh, that pen," Stephanie said. "That was the *blue* felt-tip pen. See, I need a blue pen and a black pen for the . . . the project I'm working on."

Stephanie hoped her father was buying these excuses. He'd been in his study ever since dinner, and Stephanie was going crazy, waiting for him to take a break. She just needed half a minute to swipe his phone card. But if he was going to be in his study all night, she'd never get the chance to take it!

Danny searched his desk for a black felt-tip pen. "Here you go," he said, handing the pen to her. "Now . . . do you have everything you need?"

"Yeah, Dad. Thanks." Stephanie noticed that Danny's credit card case was sticking out of his desk drawer. She was so close!

"Are you sure?" Danny asked.

"Oh, yes," she answered. "Definitely."

"Good," Danny said. "Now, can I have some uninterrupted peace and quiet? I have to finish this story outline before tomorrow morning's weekend show."

"No problem, Dad." Stephanie started for the door. This was so frustrating! She simply had to find out if her father was planning on taking a break anytime soon.

"Dad?" she asked.

Danny put his pen down again.

"Yes, Stephanie?" He sighed.

"Dad, um, do you think you'll need to take a break anytime soon?"

"I feel as if I've had lots of little breaks tonight," Danny replied. "Every time you've come to visit me, I've had to stop working. But why do you ask?"

"Well," Stephanie said, "I just thought maybe you'd help me out, because, see, I'm reorganizing my closet and I'm kind of stuck about where to put my shoes and what stuff should go on the top shelf." There! That ought to do it. Danny Tanner would never turn down anything that had to do with cleaning or reorganizing.

"Well, of course I'll help you, sweetheart," Danny said in a concerned voice. "I'd be glad to help." He looked at his watch. "Just give me half an hour in here, and then we can put up those shoe trees I bought for you last Christmas."

"Sounds great, Dad," she said. "Thanks a lot."

Stephanie had just made it back to her bedroom when she heard the telephone ring. A few seconds later Uncle Jesse called to her from downstairs.

"Stephanie! Phone for you. It's Allie."

Stephanie's heart started pounding. She was dying to talk to her best friend. And maybe Jenni had already called her. Maybe she wasn't mad anymore.

"I'll pick it up in Dad's room!" Stephanie yelled down.

On her way to the phone Stephanie ran smack into D.J.

"Oww!" Stephanie said, rubbing her shoulder. "Why don't you watch where you're going!"

"Why don't you?" D.J. retorted angrily.

"I was watching!" Stephanie shouted at her. "You're the one who ran into me!"

"I did not," D.J. protested. "You ran into me!"

Danny yanked open the door to his study. "What's all this commotion?" he said sternly. "I've about had it with you two. You've been bickering and yelling at each other for days now. What's going on?"

"D.J. ran into me!" said Stephanie.

"I did not!" D.J. shouted.

"Dad!" said Stephanie. "Can't we talk about this later? Allie's on the phone waiting for me."

Danny looked defeated. "Okay, okay, go talk to Allie. But right afterward, I want a full explanation—or you can forget about reorganizing your closet, young lady."

Stephanie ran off to get the phone. "Allie?" she said, picking up the receiver.

"About time!" Uncle Jesse said just before he hung up the downstairs extension.

"Allie?" Stephanie said again.

"Hi, Stephanie," Allie said, sounding kind of depressed.

"Allie, did Jenni talk to you? I hope you're not still mad at me. I didn't tell Adam anything. I swear!"

"Yes, Jenni Morris told me all about it. Diana was the one who talked to Adam." Allie was quiet for a moment, and then went on. "Jenni also told me what you did, Steph. Or should I say, Tabitha?"

"But didn't she tell you that it was only a joke?"

"That was pretty nasty, Stephanie. I don't care if it was only a joke. I would never have done that to you, Flamingoes or no Flamingoes."

Stephanie felt terrible. "I . . . don't know what to say—"

"Wait," Allie interrupted. "I have more to say."

Stephanie was shocked. She'd never heard Allie like this before.

"I'm really angry at you, Stephanie. I think this whole Flamingoes thing has gone to your head. You're way out of control! It's totally changed you. You're doing things you would never do if it weren't for the Flamingoes, and I don't trust any of them. Especially Jenni and Diana."

"But I talked to Jenni at lunch," Stephanie said. "She told me she'd talk to Diana. I had to make that call, Allie. It was part of the initiation. I know it was a rotten thing to do, but I was planning on calling you as soon as the initiation was over and explaining everything. I didn't know that Diana was going to say anything to Adam. I swear! But Jenni promised she would patch everything up." Then Stephanie remembered the good part. "Jenni also said that she was going to talk to you about joining the Flamingoes! Did she?"

"Yes," Allie said flatly. "She told me that the Flamingoes wanted me to try out."

"But . . . you don't sound that happy about it, Allie," Stephanie said. "I thought that's what you wanted."

"Maybe at first," Allie admitted. "But not anymore. I don't like that crowd, Stephanie. I think they're mean."

"Allie," Stephanie pleaded, "you haven't even given them a chance. Listen to me. I think if we just put up with the initiation stuff, afterward everything will be great. You should have heard Jenni in the cafeteria today, Al. She said that the Flamingoes were planning on asking you to join all along! Oh, Allie, just think of how much fun we'll have— you, me, and Darcy the only sixth-grade Flamingoes! You know, Jenni's good friends with Brandon Fallow. And Adam, too. I'm sure she'd talk to him for you."

"I think Adam's heard enough about me from the Flamingoes lately," Allie said bitterly.

"Oh, right," Stephanie said. "But it wasn't

that bad, was it, Al? And look on the bright side—at least you finally got to speak to him!"

She waited for Allie to laugh at her attempt at a joke, but Allie was silent.

"C'mon, Al," Stephanie said. "I'm really sorry about the call . . . and about everything. I know how you feel, but I never, ever meant to hurt you. Don't let Diana's big mouth get you mad at all the Flamingoes. Why don't you just give them a chance?"

Allie stood her ground. "No, Steph. I don't want to become a Flamingo. And I don't want to hang out with any Flamingoes, either!" She took a deep breath, then continued. "And that goes for hanging out with you too, if you become a Flamingo."

"What?" said Stephanie. "Is this for real?"

"You choose, Stephanie. It's either me or them."

There was complete silence on both ends of the telephone. Stephanie's mind was racing a mile a minute. Somehow everything was all messed up! And now Allie was making her choose between her friendship and the Flamingoes.

Just then, Stephanie heard her father calling.

114

"Hold on a second, Allie." Stephanie put her hand over the mouthpiece of the phone. "What, Dad?" she called.

"I'm going down to the basement to get my tools," her dad called back. "I'll meet you in your room in a few minutes."

Finally he was out of his study! Now was her chance. And maybe her *only* chance.

"Allie," Stephanie said frantically, "can . . . we talk about this later?" Oh, no! Did it sound as if she was trying to get rid of Allie? She hoped not. But she really needed to get that credit card.

"Well, I guess . . ." Allie said softly.

"Okay, I'll call you later, Al," Stephanie said. "Bye." She hung up the phone, knowing that she was going to have a lot of apologizing to do to Allie when this whole mess was over.

Stephanie figured that now was the perfect time to make her move. Quietly she slipped into her father's darkened study. The only light came from the window, and it was beginning to get dark outside. She tiptoed over to the desk, silently pulling his top desk drawer open and carefully lifting out the credit card case. But just as she was removing the phone card from the case, the overhead light snapped on.

"Stephanie!" D.J. stood in the doorway. "What are you doing with Dad's credit cards?"

Stephanie bit her bottom lip. She was going to have a tough time getting out of this one.

CHAPTER
11

◆ ◄ ◄ ◆

"Stephanie," D.J. repeated, "do you mind telling me what you're doing in here? And why are you holding Dad's phone card?"

Stephanie tried to come up with something to say, but she couldn't think of a thing.

D.J.'s expression of anger slowly turned to one of concern. "Tell me right now, Stephanie," she demanded. "Does this have anything to do with Jenni Morris?"

Stephanie was surprised. "How . . . did you know?"

D.J. came over to the desk and put a hand on her sister's shoulder. "I thought so," she said.

"Didn't I tell you not to get messed up with Jenni and that crowd?"

Stephanie shrugged.

"Steph, tell me the truth. Did Jenni dare you to steal Dad's card as part of some crazy initiation?"

Stephanie's eyes widened. Nobody knew about the dares, except Jenni and Diana. Something was terribly wrong. Her stomach began doing flip-flops. At last she nodded and quietly said, "Yes."

"I thought so," D.J. said. "This is a dirty trick Jenni learned from her obnoxious sister, Susan."

"A—a . . . trick?" Stephanie stuttered.

D.J. nodded. "It's a pretty nasty trick, Steph. You see," she went on, "Susan and her friends think they're the hot crowd at school, and they pull all these horrible pranks on unsuspecting freshmen, telling them they'll get to hang out with them if they do some harmless dares—like stealing their parents' credit cards. Then Susan and her friends charge all sorts of expensive things on the cards, but they never let the freshmen hang out with them after all. The younger girls are so scared at having stolen the cards in the first place that they never tell on Susan."

Stephanie felt her knees turn to jelly. She sank down in her father's desk chair.

"Anyway," D.J. continued, "Susan has been bragging all over school about how her little sister, Jenni, had started to trick some junior high kids lately. She's proud of it!" D.J. looked thoughtful. "But I've only heard of them having kids take department store credit cards before, not phone cards."

"Jenni's old boyfriend," croaked Stephanie weakly, putting it all together. "Mickey Parris. He moved away to Boston last month."

"That explains it," D.J. said. "I guess she could put a phone card to pretty good use." She shook her head. "Anyway, that's why I told you Darcy was crazy to have anything to do with her. I thought maybe Jenni was trying her sister's dirty tricks out on Darcy." D.J. sighed. "I guess I should have said something the other night after I saw Jenni here," she added, "but I was pretty angry at you. Also, I never thought that *you* would fall for Jenni's phoniness. I thought you'd see right through her."

Stephanie felt dizzy. Could this be true? It

could. It had to be true. D.J. wouldn't make up something like this. *And if it is true, then that means the Flamingoes were never interested in me in the first place*, Stephanie thought. *They only wanted me for my dad's credit card!*

Stephanie felt like the world's biggest fool. She also felt as if she were about to cry. Stuffing the card back into her father's card case and replacing it in the drawer, she almost threw herself into her sister's arms. Without saying any more about "I told you so," D.J. hugged her tightly as the tears started to flow.

She couldn't believe how stupid she'd been. She had fallen for the whole trick, treated her friends horribly, lied, and was just about to steal from her father. Suddenly she stopped sobbing. "Darcy!" she said to D.J. "I have to warn Darcy."

"Good thinking," said D.J.

"Steph?" Danny said, standing at the doorway holding a shoe rack, a hammer, and a screwdriver. "What's the matter, honey?"

"Stephanie has to make a really important phone call," D.J. explained for her sister. "Maybe I could help you put that shoe rack up in her closet."

Stephanie shot D.J. a grateful look.

Danny looked slightly confused and disappointed, but Stephanie knew that working in her closet would have him in a great mood in no time.

Sitting back down at her father's desk, Stephanie wiped her tears away, blew her nose, and picked up the phone. She was shaking as she dialed Darcy's number. She just hoped she could reach her before she took her parents' card.

"Stephanie, what is it?" Darcy asked when she came to the phone. "My mother said you told her it was an emergency."

"Oh, Darce! I'm so glad I caught you," Stephanie said, breathing a sigh of relief. "Listen, I need to talk to you about . . . the dares."

"The dares? But we're not supposed to talk about—"

"I know, I know," Stephanie said, not giving Darcy a chance to finish. "But we have to talk about them. It's really important."

Darcy waited to hear what her friend had to say.

Stephanie took a deep breath. "Your last dare," she began. "Was it to steal your parents' phone credit card?"

121

"Yes, it was. Yours too?"

"Darcy, I've got some bad news for you. I just found out the truth about the Flamingoes. And you're not going to like it any better than I did."

"The truth?"

"Yes. Listen, can you come over tonight? For a sleep-over?"

"Well, I guess so. Let me check." In a moment Darcy came back to the phone. "My mom can bring me over right after dinner. About eight."

"Good. When you get here, I'll explain everything."

Stephanie hung up the phone and put her head down on her father's desk. She wondered again how she could have been so stupid to get involved in such a mess. *I'm such a loser!* she thought sadly. But before the tears could come rushing back, there was one more call she had to make.

"Hello?" Allie said when she picked up the phone.

"Allie, hi . . . It's me. Listen, I wouldn't blame you if you hung up on me, but please don't."

Allie didn't say a word, but she didn't hang up, either.

Stephanie took a deep breath. "I really owe you a major apology. I can't believe what a jerk I've been. You're my best friend in the entire world, and I've just been so caught up in the whole Flamingoes thing and being cool, I kind of forgot about what was really important for a few days."

"Yeah," Allie said. "I know."

"Allie, I promise to never, ever let it happen again. Can you forgive me?"

"Well, that depends. Are you joining the Flamingoes?"

"No way!" Stephanie blurted out. "Absolutely not. I wouldn't join their stupid club if they *begged* me. Even if they sent Brandon Fallow over to my house . . . with flowers . . . I still wouldn't join!"

Allie giggled softly. "What happened?"

"It's a long story," Stephanie replied. "And I want to tell it to you. Is there any chance you can come for a sleep-over tonight? Darcy's mom said she could, and it would be really great if it could be all three of us."

Allie asked her father, and he agreed to the sleep-over plan.

"Great," said Stephanie. "See you around eight. We've got lots to talk about."

Feeling happier than she had in days, Stephanie went back into her room, where her father was standing proudly beside her newly renovated closet.

"There you go, sweetheart," he said. "A place for everything and everything in its place."

"Thanks, Dad," said Stephanie. She was touched to see that he'd even put in a special little rack for her red cowboy boots. She vowed to start wearing them tonight.

After Danny left the room, D.J. turned to her sister. "I'm sorry this stuff with the Flamingoes happened, Steph," she said. "It must have hurt a lot to find all this out at once."

"You're not kidding." Stephanie picked up Doggie Dog from the bookshelf and flopped down on her bed, hugging her old friend to her chest. "It's just that I really thought Jenni and the Flamingoes liked me. They kept telling me how cool I was and what a perfect Flamingo I was going to make."

"I guess that's all part of their act," D.J. said.

"Yeah, well, now I know she just wanted a

phone card number so she could call Mickey. Jenni never cared about me." Stephanie looked at her sister. "I didn't think anyone cared about me," she added, "not even you."

"You know that's not true, Steph," D.J. said. "Of course I care about you."

"Do you really?" Stephanie asked. "Lately you haven't wanted to hang out with me at all." Stephanie felt the tears coming again, and she didn't try to stop them. "You've been spending every possible second with Steve and totally ignoring me."

D.J. looked shocked. "But we do things together," she pointed out. "What about last Wednesday, when we rented all those horror videos and scared Joey out of his mind?"

"Yeah, but then Steve came over and you didn't want to watch anymore," Stephanie reminded her. "And I was stuck watching the rest of the movies with Michelle. You know what it's like to watch a movie with Michelle? It's impossible. She asks about a trillion questions.

"It's not that I don't like Steve," Stephanie continued. "I mean, I think he's great." She hugged Doggie Dog even closer. "I know I'll never have a boyfriend as great as Steve. I can't

125

even get any guys at school to notice I'm alive. I'll never be as popular with the guys as you are."

"That's not true, Stephanie," D.J. said softly. "Hey, you've totally forgotten about me and Jeremy Richards, haven't you?"

Stephanie thought for a minute, then a small grin appeared on her tear-streaked face. "Oh, yeah," she said. "That guy with the skateboard you were so crazy about."

"Right," D.J. said. "That stupid skateboard got closer to Jeremy than I ever did! But the point is, he was the first boy I ever sort of dated. And I was in the seventh grade then—a whole year older than you are now. Don't you remember how I cried every night for three months because he wouldn't ask me out? Then, when he finally did, I had the worst time in my entire life! He spent the whole night at the movies throwing food and shooting soda at his stupid friends in the first row. It was a total disaster.

"Anyway," D.J. continued, "I think you should just give it time, Steph. I'm sure you'll have a boyfriend before long—you're much more outgoing than I ever was. Funnier and smarter, too."

Stephanie shook her head, not convinced.

"Listen, I'm sorry if I've left you out of things lately," D.J. added. "It's just that sometimes when I'm with Steve—I'd like it to be just me and Steve. And in this house, that can be a real problem."

"Yeah, but—" Stephanie began.

"Wait a minute," D.J. said. "Before you say anything, I have an idea. What if we make one night a week for just the two of us—a Sisters Only Night? We can do whatever you want, one night a week—just me and you. No Steve, no Michelle, no anybody else. That would be kind of fun, wouldn't it?"

Stephanie grinned. "That sounds awesome, D.J.," she said. "We could go bowling, or rent a movie, or just stay home and talk about guys. Just the two of us. But . . ." Stephanie raised a finger in the air. "Do you think you could survive without Steve for one whole night?"

"Yeah, I think I could manage." D.J. smiled. "I know you have plans with Allie and Darcy later, but what if we had a little preview of Sisters Only Night right now? I have some really cool outfits for you to try on—and the perfect denim shirt to go with your new cowboy boots.

You'll look so totally hot, you'll knock the sweat socks off all those eighth-grade guys!" D.J. stood up. "Meet me in my room in twenty minutes . . . for a complete Stephanie Tanner fashion show!"

As her sister ran out of the room, Stephanie gave Doggie Dog a big kiss. Everything was going to be okay. She and her big sister were friends again, and her life was at least halfway back to normal.

CHAPTER
12

◆ ◀ ◆ ◆

Darcy was sprawled across Stephanie's bed, looking at a photograph in a magazine and trying to decide whether or not to cut her hair in bangs. Allie sat at the head of Michelle's bed, painting her toenails bright orange. And Stephanie was on the foot of her sister's bed, just lolling around with her two best friends.

Suddenly there was a knock at the door, and before Stephanie could get up, the door opened.

"It's pizza man," Danny said as he carried in a large cardboard box containing the pepperoni, sausage, double-cheese pizza the girls had ordered.

"Dad!" Stephanie exclaimed. "I can't believe

it. You're actually going to let us eat food up here in my room?"

Danny looked skeptical, but he nodded. "D.J. talked me into this," he said, still looking puzzled. "She said it was some sort of a celebration for the three of you, and you needed a special treat, so here it is. Go to it, girls." Danny set the box down on Stephanie's desk. "Now, I've brought lots of napkins, and I expect you to use them. Don't throw any garbage in the wastebaskets up here; just put it in the pizza box and carry it down to the kitchen. If anything should spill, just—"

"Dad," Stephanie interrupted him, "I think we can handle eating a pizza up here without any more instructions."

Danny gave a funny half smile and turned to leave the room.

Just as he was going out the door, Darcy shouted, "Whoops!"

Danny whirled around to see what had spilled as the three girls called out in unison, "Just kidding!"

While Darcy put the pizza slices on paper plates, Stephanie said, "I'm really, really, really sorry, Allie. I hope you're not mad. The whole situation with Jenni and Diana just got totally out of hand."

"Yeah," Darcy chimed in. "You were right about them all along, Al. They are major trouble."

"Would you guys stop apologizing already?" Allie pleaded. "This is the fourth time tonight."

Stephanie and Darcy laughed. Darcy had called Allie before dinner to apologize and had begged forgiveness three times since they got to Stephanie's house.

Allie took the slice Stephanie handed her and added, "Anyway, there's no harm done, really," she said. "I mean, I'll eventually get over the whole Adam Green thing—when I'm about thirty-five!" She made a face. "But you haven't told me yet what happened to make you change your minds about Jenni and Diana."

Stephanie groaned loudly. "Well, it's a long story," she said, "but I'm happy to say that thanks to D.J., it's a story that is not going to get any longer."

"What are you talking about, Steph?" Allie asked.

Stephanie took a deep breath and began to explain about how Jenni and Diana had set them up from the very beginning. She told about the top secret three dares and finished up with Jenni's little phone card scheme.

When she'd heard everything, Allie exclaimed, "That's awful!"

"You're telling us," Darcy said.

"I was so lucky that D.J. caught me taking my dad's card," Stephanie went on. "And that she just knew Jenni Morris was involved somehow."

"So are things back to normal between you and D.J. now?" Allie asked.

"Better than normal," Stephanie said. "Everything's great. We talked it all out. We're not mad at each other anymore. And," she added, "I'm glad you're not mad anymore, Allie. I'm really, really, *really* glad."

"Hey!" Darcy exclaimed as she licked a long string of cheese from her finger. "I just had an idea. What if we started our own club? Just the three of us."

"That is an *awesome* idea," Allie agreed. "We can have our own sleep-overs and our own club meetings."

"Yeah, and our own friendship bracelets and trademark color," Stephanie added.

Darcy was thoughtful. "But what will we call ourselves?" she asked. Then she started laughing. "What about the Pelicans? Or the Peacocks?"

Stephanie and Allie laughed.

"How about the Purple Parrots?" Stephanie offered, cracking everyone up.

"No!" Allie was laughing so hard, she could barely talk "I've got it . . . the Whooping Cranes."

Stephanie doubled over. "Or wait!" she screamed. "What about the Crazy Cuckoos?"

"No, no!" Allie said breathlessly. "The Goose Gals!"

"The Goose Gals?" Darcy repeated, laughing hysterically. "Now, that's bad!"

"Not as bad as the Birdbrains," Allie pointed out happily.

"Wait, wait, wait," Stephanie said. "Seriously, can I make a good suggestion? Why don't we forget about naming our club? We don't need a dumb bird name—we can just do things together, as best friends. The sleep-overs, the meetings, all of it. We don't have to name ourselves. We don't have to prove our loyalty to anyone other than ourselves."

"I agree," Darcy said. Then she cleared her throat. "I vote for no club name."

"I second that motion," Allie chirped. "And I vote we have our first meeting of the No Name Club tomorrow at the frozen yogurt shop at the mall—my treat."

"Hold it," Darcy said suddenly. "The Flamingoes are meeting at the mall tomorrow. What if we run into them?"

For a moment none of the girls spoke. And then Stephanie piped up. "So what?" she said. "We're not going to let the Flamingoes tell us what to do or what *not* to do. The mall's a big place—and the Flamingoes don't own it."

"That sounds great, guys," Allie said happily. "Frozen yogurt at the mall."

"And if we do happen to run into a Flamingo," Darcy added, "we can just say . . ."

And all the girls finished her sentence together: "Catch ya later!"

"And with any luck," Stephanie said, "it'll be much, *much* later."

An all-new series of novels based on your
favorite character from the hit TV series!

FULL HOUSE™
Stephanie

Phone Call From a Flamingo

The Boy-Oh-Boy Next Door

Twin Troubles

Hip Hop Till You Drop

Here Comes the Brand-New Me

The Secret's Out

AND LOOK FOR NEW ADVENTURES
COMING IN 1995!

Available from Minstrel® Books
Published by Pocket Books

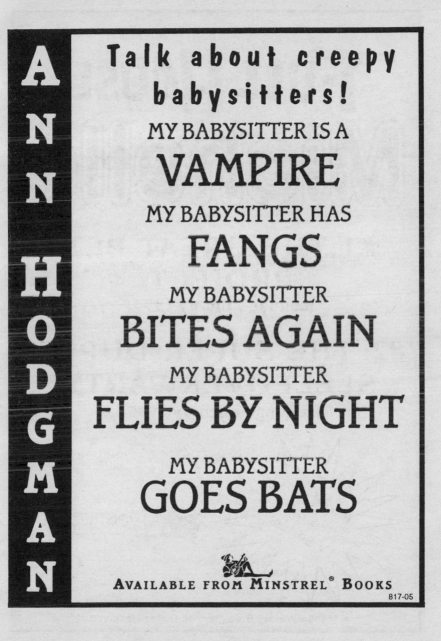

FULL HOUSE™
Michelle

#1: THE GREAT PET PROJECT
(coming January 1995)

#2: THE SUPER-DUPER SLEEPOVER PARTY
(coming February 1995)

Based on the Hit TV Series!

A MINSTREL® BOOK